ALADDIN
SINS BAD

ALADDIN SINS BAD

THE ALADDIN TRILOGY #2

J. R. RAIN
PIERS ANTHONY

Aladdin Sins Bad

Copyright © 2011 by J. R. Rain and Piers Anthony

All rights reserved.

License Notes

ISBN: 1500676314

ISBN 13: 9781500676315

OTHER BOOKS BY PIERS ANTHONY AND J.R. RAIN

ALADDIN SINS BAD

Author's Note: This novel was suggested by the adventures of Sinbad the Sailor in the Arabian Nights. I (Piers Anthony) have six translations of those adventures, which are summarized by Sinbad in Chapter One. Sinbad's wife died of natural causes and was placed in the underground tomb, along with her surviving husband, Sinbad, as was the custom in that culture. He managed to find his way out and returned home. But suppose she was not really dead, but only enchanted by some fell nemesis who used this as a device to lure our heroes into a trap? We went on from there, as you have seen.

We are indebted to Rudy Reyes, who proofread the manuscript and found a score of errors I had overlooked. Or, as I like to put it, typos grow on the page after the proofreading. They didn't know there would be a second proofing to catch them. It was a trap, see...

—Piers Anthony

CHAPTER ONE

"You're what?" I demanded, stunned.

"I am with child," Jewel replied. "I knew I shouldn't have cured your impotence. That led to nothing but mischief."

Suddenly it made sense: she was pregnant! That was great news in a couple of respects. First it meant I would have a blood-heir again. Second it explained her recent difficult strangeness. She had taken to eating odd things, and her moods had become perplexing. "That's great," I said weakly.

"Naturally I will not be catering to you in bed for the duration," she said. "I need to protect the baby. You will have to be satisfied with concubines."

"But I'm impotent with concubines!" I protested. "You're the only one I can make it with." I had been impotent following the deaths of my original wife and son, until Jewel took me in hand, as it were. It was love I had needed.

"I'm sure you can make do if you really try."

I loved her, but she was at times the daughter of a dog. She knew I could not be unfaithful to her, even with alternates she approved.

A courtier approached. "Sire, the sailor is back."

"Sailor?" asked Jewel. "What sailor?"

"Sinbad the sailor, your highness."

Her eyes widened with pleasure, a look normally reserved for me in the royal bedroom. I frowned at her reaction, but hers was a common one. Sinbad was famous far and wide for his travels and, from what I understood, had garnered quite a reputation with the ladies. I was instantly jealous, but I bit my tongue.

"He is here, then?" she asked, and actually waved her face with her hand.

I bit down a little harder.

The courier, looking slightly perplexed, since he had come to see me, after all, said, "Yes, your highness. Here to see King Aladdin about a business proposal."

Jewel turned to me. "Then we are done here, my husband. Go attend to your guest."

Her eyes flared brightly again, then she gave me a peck on the cheek and departed.

As if I didn't have enough on my mind already. Sinbad the Sailor had been petitioning for an audience for months. I had put him off without an audience because I knew what he wanted: a ship to go adventuring in. Ships were expensive, and the man had already lost several. He was not a good risk. Sure, he would promise to deliver half the fortune he made to the kingdom. But if he lost the ship, as he probably would, that would come to nothing.

And my wife's obvious interest in the man didn't help his cause.

What the Hades. It was time to put an end to this nonsense. I would make a suitable pretense of kingly fairness, hear the man out, then explain courteously why it was impossible to oblige his request and send him away forever. It was better than being constantly pestered. So he wouldn't take no from a subordinate? He'd take it from the king, or lose his head, literally.

Then I had a notion. "Fetch Duban."

The courier bowed. "I will summon the Crown Prince," he agreed.

Duban was Jewel's son, now rising onto age twelve, whom I had officially adopted when I married her. He was a good boy, and a truly potent magician. Both were problems: a nice boy would have trouble doing the necessary as king, and his magic had not been much in evidence lately. He needed discipline, and it was my job to provide it. His doting mother wouldn't.

In moments Duban was there before me. "Sire," he said formally.

"Come with me," I said curtly. "I have a situation to deal with, and you need to learn how it's done if you're going to be an effective king some day."

"I don't want to be any kind of king," he said. "I'm not the kind. I lack hard-minded discipline."

At least he was realistic. "You will learn it. Even if you're not king, it will do you good to know how to deal with people."

"Can't I leave that to my woman, as you do?"

Ouch! It was true that Jewel provided the backbone for handling routine that I sometimes lacked. "A man needs to be able to do it himself. Then he can leave it to others if he wishes. I'm sure Myrrh will help you when the time comes."

"She can read my mind!" he wailed.

Which was true. Myrrh, now eleven years old, was a truly talented girl who had helped rescue Duban from evil captivity. She was a mind reader who could sometimes see the future. That was why we banned her from the royal chambers at night. I could see how it could be awkward for a boy verging on manhood, even if he was bound to marry her when adult.

"You know," I said, "I suspect that you and I might do well to go away somewhere for a while, get to know each other better. Away from the women."

"Yes," he agreed thoughtfully. "I love Mother, but sometimes she smothers me."

"I'll keep it in mind. Maybe I can find a spot mission where women aren't welcome."

"Maybe then I could work on my magic."

We arrived at the audience chamber. There was a somewhat scruffy man I knew immediately was Sinbad the Sailor. "Sire," he said, bowing low.

3

I took my throne, and Duban took a chair, dispensing with further formalities. "Yes, I am Aladdin, and this is Crown Prince Duban. What's on your mind, sailor?"

He came right to the point. "Sire, I want a ship."

I frowned. "Ships do not grow on trees. Why do you want a ship?"

"To garner fabulous riches, all of which you may take for the kingdom."

"Why should I risk a valuable ship for a mere half of the take?" Then I paused, frowning. "How much did you say?"

"You can have it all, Sire. I care not for riches."

This was not following the script. "You've always amassed riches before. What's different this time?"

"I want to rescue my wife."

Both Duban and I stiffened. If this was a personal motive, it was difficult to disparage. "I did not know you were married."

"That's because I wasn't, or so I thought. I thought my wife was dead. But recently I received information that she lives, but is captive. I must gather great riches to redeem her."

Duban picked up on this. "So the voyage is to give riches to someone else, not this kingdom."

Sinbad actually fidgeted. "There should be enough for both. I know where great treasures are."

"Where?" I asked, thinking he would balk.

Instead he launched into a summary of his several prior voyages. "When I first sailed, we landed on an isle that turned out to be a great fish, and I got dumped in the water and barely survived. Now I know that fish was a whale, from which we could get valuable ambergris. On my second, we encountered great roc birds and huge serpents, but also fabulous diamonds. On my third, a cyclops who surely had obscene treasure hidden away. On my fourth I met and married my wife, a treasure beyond reckoning. On my fifth, a wretched old man who sought to ride me to death, as he had others; there should be valuables hidden there, from those who died. On my sixth, I found myself

4

in a cave with rubies, and later found emeralds and pearls. On my seventh, an elephant graveyard where there are great quantities of ivory. All I need is a ship to gather them. After I redeem my wife, I can return to fetch similar treasures to take back to Samarkand."

This was a wild story, surely exaggerated, surely not worth believing, let alone risking a ship for. But my eye caught Duban's eye. This just might be a pretext to get away from the women for a while, and maybe see some interesting sights along the way.

Except for one thing: I always got horribly seasick on a ship. Did I want to get away that much?

CHAPTER TWO

I nearly ordered Sinbad away. Nearly.

Instead, I told him to return on the morrow and I would give him my final decision. He bowed graciously, his robust beard just scraping the polished tile of the greeting room. He exited the hall quickly, clearly knowing when not to push his luck, which showed a rare level of awareness and common sense. At least, rare in my experience. The stories of Sinbad had reached even me, and it is a wonder the man is alive; that is, if his tales could be believed. After all, he often returned alone from his fantastic voyages, so there was little corroborative evidence. Still, I always fancied myself a good judge of men—indeed, I was due to preside over the royal court shortly—and something told me that Sinbad was an honest-enough ruffian.

"Did he say cyclops, Faddy?" I whispered.

I felt an invisible presence manifest next to me, a surge of energy that made the hair rise on my arms, and in an instant my ifrit was by my side.

"Indeed he did, master." The voice was spoken lightly, directly into my ear. Despite being surrounded by guards, courtesans and general palace staff, his presence was known only to me.

"Have you ever seen such a creature?"

"They are legendary, even in Djinnland. Then again, so is Sinbad. It is a rare honor to meet such an acclaimed adventurer."

I bristled, mildly irked. I felt a wave of rare jealousy. "You mean acclaimed *wrecker of ships*," I said, grumbling. "He is just as famous for coming home empty-handed, and how do we know his tales are even true?"

"There is but one way to find out," said Faddy.

I knew what he was getting at. Indeed, already all signs were pointing for a fantastic voyage, but I was hesitant. Leaving for the high seas while a wife is newly with child is not a decision I would make lightly, or even one I looked forward discussing with a wife who lately was moody and temperamental at best.

"Sire," said Faddy. "Have you given thought to my request?"

"Your request is highly unusual, ifrit," I said.

I sensed him fading away and had a brief, mental image of the tall being bowing low. "Yes, sire. Thank you for your consider—"

"Wait, El Fadl," I said, using the ifrit's formal name. "I have given thought to your most unusual request, and I have decided…to release you."

"Master?"

"You're a free man. Or djinn."

And in that instant, the tall ifrit appeared by my side, to the shock of those around us, most of who gasped, although one or two screamed. One guard actually fainted, slumping forward and just missing impalement by his own spear.

Faddy bowed low again, and when he looked up at me, there were tears of joy on his strangely handsome face. I say strangely, because it was obvious the ifrit was not of this world. His chin was too pointy, as were his ears. But the joy on his face was universal.

"Thank you, master."

"I am not your master, Faddy."

"Thank you, sire. I cannot express to you the joy I feel. What made you change your mind? Any king would want his own ifrit."

Indeed. Faddy had come in handy in more ways than one. As a secret spy, he was irreplaceable, but I also prided myself on being a fair and equal ruler, and to have a being bound to me against his will did not set well with me. He had asked for his freedom, having had a taste of such freedom on a recent adventure to Djinnland, and now Faddy was not to be denied, as

I suspected would be the case. He hungered for freedom, as he had expressed to me days ago, and I would not deny my ifrit his heart's desires.

"What will you do with yourself, Fadl?" I asked. "Now that you are free to do as you wish."

The tall being stood straight and wiped away his tears. Others in the court continued staring at him. Despite rumors of my magical lamp, the sudden appearance of a magical being was not commonplace in Agrabah, my kingdom.

"I seek a mate, sire."

"A female djinn?"

"Of course. I have no interest in humans." Faddy actually made a face.

I chuckled. "I was unaware of the existence of female djinns."

"They exist, or so I have heard. I shall devote my life to finding a mate."

"Then I bid thee well, my friend. Do not be a stranger."

Faddy smiled, bowed again, and faded away. The guard nearby, who had just recovered enough to push himself up to his knees, caught sight of the disappearing djinn, and promptly pitched forward again.

———

"She is a witch!" hissed a young woman. "I have seen her turn staffs into snakes."

"I see," I said. "Did anyone else see this staff turn into a snake?"

"Yes!" shouted the four accusers in unison, but when questioned separately, they all described the snake differently. I was beginning to have my doubts.

The accused stood before me, her head bowed, listening to the accusations leveled against her. She was quite old, with back bowed. She had yet to speak, even as her four accusers presented wild tales of witchcraft.

"Esteemed woman," I said when I had heard enough, "what say you for yourself?"

She looked up at me now for the first time. "I am not a witch, my lord, but I do see things."

"What kind of things?"

"Future things. Visions."

"You see, my lord!" screamed one of her accusers. "Who but a witch sees future things? Only Allah knows the future!"

"Quiet!" I said, raising my voice only slightly. Had I raised my voice another octave, the man who spoke out of turn would have been dragged from my court. I looked back at the elderly woman. "These visions you have, have any of them come to pass?"

"All of them, my liege. Every one of them."

"Do any of them concern me?"

"Ah, the ego of kings. Yes, my liege, one does concern you, and it is the reason why I'm here today."

"You are here today because you have been accused of witchcraft."

"No, my lord. I am here today because I was not granted an audience with you."

"I do not understand."

"Twice I have come to see you, my liege, and twice I have been turned away."

I blinked, feeling my anger rising. "So your accusers do not think you a witch?"

"Oh they do, my lord."

I glanced at her four accusers, who ranged from young to old, three men and one woman. They looked as perplexed as I felt.

The old woman said, "I have a bit of a reputation, my lord, and so when I was turned away by your guards, I spread stories about me, stories about staffs turning into snakes, and well water turning to blood."

"And none of this is true?"

She gave me a small grin. "Of course not, my lord."

"And so you did all of this to gain an audience with me?"

"Yes, my lord."

I sat back and studied her. "You have gone to great lengths to speak to me."

"Yes."

I motioned to those in attendance who were chattering excitedly to each other. "You have turned my court into a farce."

"That was not my intent, my lord."

"And what is your intent?"

"To save your life, my lord."

"To save it how?"

"By begging you not to go on this sea voyage."

I sat forward. "What sea voyage?"

"The sea voyage you have been pondering."

I opened my mouth to speak, but words failed me. If she indeed had the Sight, it would do little to question her about how she came to know of the voyage. Instead, I ordered her into my private chamber, and when we were alone, I said, "Tell me more about your vision."

"It is a trap, my Lord."

"A trap how?"

"The one who seeks your kingdom has gone to great lengths to destroy you."

"Who?" I asked, although I had a fair idea who this might be.

She shook her head. "All is not revealed to me, my lord, but I do know that if you continue with this adventure, you will perish and your kingdom will be in ruins, but—"

"But what?"

"No, I should not speak it."

"Speak, woman. I command it."

"Yes, my lord. There is, however, a small chance of success."

I frowned. "Just a small chance?"

She nodded. "I have also seen you return triumphantly, your enemy forever vanquished, surrounded in more jewels and gold than any man could ever dream. But this outcome is highly unlikely, sire. More than likely, you will meet a fate worse than death."

I thanked her for her time and dismissed her. And as I sat alone in my chamber, silently brooding on this usual turn of events, I came to a decision.

Allah, help me, but I came to a decision.

CHAPTER THREE

"Are you out of what little mind you have?" Jewel demanded. "Only an utter idiot with a brain clot would pull a stunt like that!"

I merely looked at her.

She had to smile. "I walked into that one, didn't I? I described you all too well. Well, if I can't stop you, I might as well wish you well. At least you'll have Faddy along to guide you. It will give Duban some practice learning how to run a kingdom."

"I freed Faddy. I'm taking Duban with me. It will be a coming-of-age experience for him."

Her prior blowout had been like a fierce wind storm. Now it was as if a volcano erupted in the palace, trying to blow the roof off. I waited, trusting that it would pass in time. Finally she vented most of her steam, and a certain dark canniness manifested. That made me nervous. She was up to something.

"Well, let's see what my son has to say about this," she said with faux calm.

"Duban," I said, just loudly enough for him to hear me in the adjacent chamber. He had of course been near, and stayed clear; he knew his mother as well as I did.

He came to join me. "I want to do it, Mother."

"I can't possibly let you risk your royal posterior on such a mad venture. It's too dangerous."

"I have encountered danger before, Mother." That was the understatement of the year. An evil demon had sought to make him a human sacrifice, and nearly succeeded.

"Well, not this time. I forbid it."

"I answer to the king."

She stared at him, astonished. "Are you defying me, Duban?"

Duban made a placating gesture. "Why Mother, I would never do that. But someone needs to help see to the safety of the king, who as we know is an utter idiot with a brain clot, and perhaps I can serve. It will also enable me to practice my independence and my magic."

The emotions of fury and pride warred openly on her face: anger at me, pride in her son, who was showing some gumption. She could say no to me, having little or no respect for my status as king of Agrabah, but not to her son. She knew, on some deep secret level, that a mother's boy would not make the best king.

She tried another tack. "I wonder what Myrrh thinks of this?"

Myrrh appeared as if summoned, as she surely had been, mentally. She was an increasingly pretty girl of eleven, with dark eyes and lustrous long dark hair, on the verge of nubility. She could make Duban do anything she wanted, but had the grace not to show it in public. "I think they're both crazy. A seer predicted that it would be a disaster."

"You have some sighting ability yourself," I said to Myrrh. Now for the clincher. Phrasing was everything. "Tell us: which way is disaster more likely: if I go alone, or with Duban?" Not whether I went or stayed home, which would have wiped out my prospects.

She had to answer, however reluctantly. "If you go alone, sire."

"Traitor," Jewel muttered. But her heart was no longer in it; she realized she had been outmaneuvered. "We'd better roust up some seasick medicine for our heroes. A cartload of ginger should do."

And so we won the seeming approval of the ladies, and made plans for our voyage of adventure. As a safety precaution we assumed aliases: Niddala for me, Nabud for him, our names backwards. There would be no announcement of the king's departure; as far as the kingdom knew, the king and crown prince remained in Samarkand, issuing orders the queen dutifully relayed. Were truth known, Jewel rather liked the prospect of ruling the kingdom for a while without having to handle the middleman. What had that middleman accomplished, after all, other than getting her pregnant?

Meanwhile Sinbad, granted a half-share of the enterprise by royal dispensation, soon lined up several minor local merchants to finance the other half. Among these was Niddala and his twelve year old nephew. Our interest was in ambergris, and we accepted Sinbad's assurance that he knew where to find it. It would be the ship's very first call.

First we had to get to the coast. We got fit horses and rode south with a caravan several days. That gave Duban nice travel experience, which he liked. He was becoming an accomplished rider. Sinbad and I just wanted to get there, but Duban enjoyed the ride itself.

The ship was a small old merchanter named the Stout Prospect, more familiarly by the crew as Fat Chance. She was a distinctly unassuming vessel, a single-masted lateen-rigged dhow, obviously nothing a king would board. But she was tight, her hold was capacious, and her small crew was competent. It really wasn't her fault that newer, larger ships had absconded with most of the trade, leaving her to have to resort to renting out for less desirable missions.

Our cabin was tiny; there was barely room for the two of us under the high poop deck. I gulped down some of the seasick glop the moment we boarded, but still felt green under the chin. Duban, fortunately, did not have a problem.

We set sail at dawn. The captain shouted orders, the yardarm lifted, and the triangular sail was hauled into place. They angled it to catch the wind and we were off. I managed not to throw up too often. I could see that the other merchants held me in contempt, so I did not try to socialize with them at meals. I wasn't hungry anyway. What kind of a merchant got seasick? Surely a poor one.

Then a merchant approached me. He was portly and evinced no sign of sickness, cursed be his solid posterior. "Niddala, eh? I have heard that name before."

Oh, no! Had he caught on to my identity as the king? "I've been around," I said cautiously.

"Now I've got it! A spook-for-hire in the western region. I wondered what happened to him."

What a relief! "Now I am a merchant," I said.

"I heard some fancy beautiful woman hired him, and they disappeared."

"I'm still working for her," I said.

"That figures. I'd risk sickness too, for a creature like that."

"She wants ambergris."

He shook his head. "It's a fool's mission."

"She's even prettier nude."

"Ah. Of course." He moved on, understanding. Any man was a fool for a lovely woman. Especially one who adorned her demands with favors.

Duban had the wit to make no comment.

A century or two later, or so it seemed, we furled the sail beside a small island. Duban and I went to see what was going on. Why were we not proceeding toward our destination?

"Do not set foot on that isle," Sinbad said with a smile. "It will not remain there long."

Then there was a plume of vapor from one end of the isle, and it sank under the water. It was a whale! We had arrived!

I had of course boned up on ambergris. It was black waxy stuff with a bad smell. It was formed in the intestines of sperm whales, probably a product of their indigestion. There was a rarer harder gray variant that was far more precious, but was generally locked inside the whale, almost impossible to get out. Naturally women liked to put the stuff on their faces. "There will be blobs of it floating in the water," I said with authority. "Or washed ashore. We have merely to find them."

But there were no blobs. An old mariner knew why: "The natives have discovered its value. They patrol constantly and salvage any they find. You will need to purchase it from them. Unfortunately they know they have a captive market; perfumeries and medicant makers are desperate for ambergris. They charge high."

That annoyed Sinbad. "We'll not do business with legalized robbers. We'll find our own."

"I wish you success," the mariner said with heavy irony.

"Let's go ashore and ask around," I suggested to Duban. "We might learn something."

"Of course, Uncle," he agreed. He knew that I just wanted to get off the pitching ship for a while, to settle my roiling stomach.

Sinbad obligingly furnished a lifeboat and joined us in the tiny craft. He and I rowed while Duban steered.

Ashore we soon learned what we were up against. The locals garnered only about half the ambergris. The rest was sucked away by a whirlpool that formed when the tide went out. All manner of floating refuse entered it, including much ambergris, and sometimes even a whale, but none came out. The whirlpool led to some subterranean chamber that did not like to disgorge its acquisitions.

"There is surely a fortune in ambergris in that underwater cave," Sinbad said. "If only we could get it out."

"We can probably reach it," I said. "All we need is to guide our little craft into the whirlpool when it forms, and it will take us there."

Both Sinbad and Duban looked at me, not sharing the joke. If we rode the whirlpool down, we would come to look much like blobs of ambergris ourselves.

"Maybe if we build a capsule," I suggested. "That would float on the water, and be drawn in by the whirlpool. We could ride in it, buffered by pillows, and open it when it comes to rest. That's bound to be where the ambergris is."

"Assuming we make it safely in," Sinbad said. "How do we get out again? The whirlpool is one-way."

I pondered. "I'm working on the details," I said.

We rowed back to the ship. "You know, Nabud, a little magic here might help," I said. "How are you at reversing whirlpools?"

"I have no idea."

"Well, work on it. You need to get your magic in shape anyway."

"When it's a life and death matter, my magic comes unbidden. But at other times I can't seem to evoke it."

"Well, you need to learn to evoke it at will."

"Yes I do," he agreed. "I will keep trying."

"Let me get some more advice." I rubbed my brass ring before remembering that Faddy no longer worked for me.

To my surprise, the ifrit appeared. Rather, his voice sounded in my ear. "Master."

"What are you doing here?" I asked quietly. "I freed you. Did you forget?

"Maybe I miss your company, mortal. You get into such entertaining scrapes."

He probably wouldn't help, but as long as he was here, why not try? "We need to get safely into and out of a whirlpool. Got any ideas?"

"Many."

I bit off my irritation; the ifrit was toying with me. "Will you vouchsafe one to me?"

"Maybe."

"What are you after, you solidified cloud of smoke?"

"I no longer have to do your bidding, mortal. It behooves you to ask me politely."

Oh. He wanted respect. That griped me, but I bit the metal and made an effort. "Please, El Fadl sir, honor me with your informed opinion."

"That's better," Faddy agreed. "I will scout about and see what I come up with." His presence faded.

"Thank you," I murmured, knowing he could still hear me. Then, to the others: "I should have a notion soon."

Assuming Faddy played along.

CHAPTER FOUR

I consumed more of the ginger seasickness glop, making a face and wondering what was worse: the glop going down, or the upchuck coming up.

Sinbad, Duban and myself were sitting together in my cramped cabin. Above deck I could hear the workers laughing and drinking and enjoying the downtime as Sinbad and I decided our next move. Duban was with me, as I wanted the lad to learn the matters of men, and how we hash out courses of action. That is, with thought and foresight, and not with fists and yelling. The way of a ruler is not how loud one can raise his voice, but how well one can control his emotions.

Not to mention, I didn't want to expose the lad to the rascals above deck; after all, it was coming on evening and the drinking would soon give way to gambling or worse. Perhaps talk of loose women and exploits I would rather my son not be exposed to. At least, not yet. Besides, his mother would skin me alive if her son came back talking like a sailor.

"So how do you propose we build this vessel, my lord?" asked Sinbad. So far on this trip, Sinbad had mostly kept to himself, lost in his worry and grief. I had some inkling to what the man was going through, having lost my own wife and child years ago to a nefarious plot. And if the old seer had been even half correct, the same evil creature who had taken so much from me, had now embroiled Sinbad in a similar plot, one that threatened his own wife and that of my kingdom.

But despite his obvious pain and concern for his wife, Sinbad had a spirited sparkle to his eye that promised adventure, mischief and rare cunning. He made for a fine companion.

Now music broke out from above, string instruments and flutes, followed by whoops and claps and the pounding boots. My son's waning attention shifted from us to the raucous sounds above, as his own booted foot kept beat to the music. My stepson, I knew, had an ear for music. In fact, the best musicians in all of Samarkand had given him private lessons to the point where there was nothing left for him to learn.

Before I could answer Sinbad's question, my stepson spoke, "Father, may I go topside to...view the stars?"

"Just the stars and no more?"

He looked away. "Yes, father."

"And you do not wish to stay here and take part in our discussions?"

"I would like some fresh air, father."

"I see, and the music above has nothing to do with this decision?"

"Please, father."

"Begone, lad, and if I find you gambling you will answer to your mother."

He turned momentarily green, and not from seasickness. The threat of his mother's wrath was enough to turn anyone's insides into water. He nodded to myself and Sinbad and dashed up the short ladder and out of sight.

"Your son is a special boy," said Sinbad.

"You have no idea."

"Ah, but I do know. He has the gift."

"What gift is that, sailor?"

"I can see the magic around him, sire. It is like a soft light, glowing around him like a halo, sometimes flaring and sparking when he is excited, like it did just now."

"How do you know this?"

"Because I have it, too. But just a hint of it, truth be known, but certainly enough to recognize another, and your son...your son has rare gifts, of that you can be sure."

"You are full of surprises, sailor," I said.

"My surprises are what keep me alive. Like I said, I have enough gifts to get by. Perhaps a small distraction here, or a minor illusion there. Just enough for me to escape or attack or buy some time. The magic is not strong in me, but it has proven invaluable at times, although I rarely speak of it."

"And you speak of it now because of my son?"

"Your son, as I'm sure you are well aware, has a rare gift. The magic that surrounds him, should he learn to harness it, could move mountains. Literally. But for now, I suspect you have a different problem."

"What do you mean?"

"His love for music is greater than his love for magic...or even ruling kingdoms."

"No son of mine will be a musician," I barked.

Sinbad simply shrugged, and there was a spark in his eye. Merriment, perhaps, suggesting that he knew best. I was about to bark another retort when Faddy appeared by my side.

"Master," said the whispery voice.

Sinbad suddenly sat upright, pointing to me from across the small cabin. "You have an ifrit."

"You can see him?" I asked, surprised.

"Most certainly. It is one of my gifts, to see into the spirit world, including that of the djinn."

"Well, sailor, you are only half right. I had an ifrit." I turned my attention to Faddy. "You might as well show yourself, Smoke Face, there are no secrets here."

Bowing slightly, the ifrit appeared by my side, partially wedged between a cushion and the slanted cabin wall. In fact, part of him was inside the wall, a disconcerting sight at best.

"Honorable Sinbad, your exploits have reached even me."

Sinbad grinned broadly, his first real grin since our voyage began. "It is a pleasure, my ifrit friend."

Next to me, Faddy veritably beamed, which rankled me to no end. Had I not had my own adventures that would rival any of Sinbad's? I pushed aside the childish feeling. "What have you discovered, ifrit?"

"Discovered? What do you mean?" asked Sinbad, sitting forward.

"I gave my ex-ifrit an assignment, one that he certainly was not compelled to undertake, but which he chose to undertake anyway, for reasons that I still do not understand."

"You amuse me, Master, as I have said."

His reasoning still did not add up to me. Unless compelled, I have never heard of a case where a djinn willingly helped his human counterpart. I let it go for now.

Sinbad took all of this in with a jovial smile. His thick beard and mustache seemed particularly expressive, rising and falling easily with the smallest of grins. "And what is this assignment, if I may ask?"

The boat rocked gently in the currents. Above, I heard a change in music. One that seemed particularly skilled and melodious. I frowned at that. I said, "He was given the task to figure out how we might escape the whirlpool."

"I see!" said Sinbad, clapping. "And pray tell, my good djinn, what have you come up with?"

Above, the music picked up in tempo. There were more hoots and hollering, whistles and stomping of the feet. I think men were dancing. I frowned some more, knowing my son was up there.

"I'm afraid your king, the venerable Aladdin, has not been entirely forthcoming with you," said Faddy. "He has yet another djinn, one far more powerful than I. In fact, some claim perhaps the most powerful of all."

"Prince Zeyn might have something to say about that," I said, mentioning the cruel djinn who had destroyed my family so long ago, and who might also be behind Sinbad's own troubles.

"And where is this djinn that you speak of?" asked Sinbad.

"The djinn that I speak of is in a safe place," I said, frowning at Faddy. Lamprey, my nickname for the powerful djinn who had been in my care all these years, was my closely guarded secret. Or, had been my secret. "What's gotten into you, ifrit?"

"You asked for my help, my liege, and I'm giving it."

"I did not ask you to give away my secrets. If you do so again, your presence will not be welcome."

"Understood, master."

"I'm most certainly not your master," I said. "And if you continue giving away my secrets, you will no longer be a friend either. Got it, Smoke Face?"

"As you wish, my master."

"Your djinn," said Sinbad wildly. "He can help rescue my wife!"

"Perhaps," I said, "but first we need more information."

"But if your djinn is as powerful as you say, then you can just command him to rescue my wife!"

Faddy said, "Allow me, master. Aladdin's djinn and the mighty Prince Zeyn are of near equal strength. If Prince Zeyn is behind your wife's disappearance, there will be dark magic surrounding her indeed. Magic that Lamprey cannot easily undo."

"This Lamprey, can he then help us recover treasure?"

"He would," I said, "if I would allow it."

"And you will not allow it?"

"And let a djinn live my life?" I bellowed, slapping the sailor heartily on the shoulder. "Where is the adventure in that, man?"

"I don't want adventure, my liege. I want my wife."

Except I didn't believe it. I saw the fire erupt behind Sinbad's eyes. He was indeed a man of action.

Faddy continued, "There is more. One old man claimed that the whirlpool led to a land of the walking dead."

"I do not understand," I said.

Sinbad nodded, "Aye. I have heard such a tale, but I did not know it was here. The isle of the damned." He turned to Faddy. "So it is here, beneath the whirlpool?"

Faddy nodded gravely, although I caught a hint of a smirk on his narrow lips. Already he was beginning to fade. "You have with you two great magicians, my liege. I suggest, once you have located the ambergris, you utilize one of them and make haste. They say those who journey to the land of the damned never return."

"Begone!" I said irritably. Faddy, of late, was becoming an irritant. I should never have freed him, or permitted his return.

The music above hit a high note, followed by much clapping, and I moved quickly out of the cabin and up the rickety ladder. There, encircled by mostly drunken sailors, was my son playing a lyre. Men of all shapes and sizes and sobriety danced around him. Clapping and keeping beat to the beautiful music that issued from his instrument.

My anger abated when I saw the joy on my stepson's face.

I knew then that he would never be king.

I slipped below deck again, where Sinbad and I made plans for our covered vessel...and our journey to the land of the dead.

CHAPTER FIVE

"Here are the rules of the road," I told Sinbad firmly. "No special magic unless it's absolutely unavoidable. I believe that anything magic can accomplish can also be accomplished without magic, albeit it maybe less conveniently. It's no good to depend on magic; it makes a man grow fat and useless."

Sinbad shook his head. "The main reason I haven't used magic is that I have not had enough of it to use. How are we going to deal with walking dead if we don't use magic? I have heard that they long to consume living human flesh, thinking it will make them live again."

I had heard similar. Also that they could not be killed, being already dead. It was said that the only way to stop a zombie from attacking was to hack it into fragments too small to move effectively, and even then the fragments would strive to reform into zombies and resume the attack. I did not have a formal list of things I did not want to do, but fighting zombies hand to hand was surely near the top of it.

But we needed to fetch the ambergris. That meant dealing with the zombies. "There must be a way."

Sinbad gazed at me cannily. He was not a foolish man, and he already knew better than to try to thwart my notions openly. "Maybe this compromise: no magic until such time as we are about to be chomped to death and become zombies ourselves."

I hesitated, not enamored of any loophole. Who was to judge how close to chomping we might be?

"What would your wife the queen say if your son got chomped when you could have prevented it?"

"Camel turds!" I swore. "All right, I accept the compromise." Because even my becoming a walking dead zombie would scarcely dissuade Jewel from wreaking vengeance on me.

However, thereafter my mind focused. "A boat on a boat," I said. "Top one upside down, sealed tight to make a waterproof capsule with only holes for the oars, and plenty of grease to stop leakage there. We'll ride the whirlpool down, and lift the top boat when we come safely to rest."

"That may do, one-way," Sinbad said. "But what of the return?"

"It's a tidal whirlpool, existing only when the tide goes out. There is surely a similar whirlpool on the other side, existing only when the tide comes in. We'll ride that out, in due course."

"That's so utterly crazy it just might work!"

"Thank you."

"And what about the zombies?"

"I'm working on that. Meanwhile we can assemble the boats."

We assembled the boats: two matched landing craft, precisely fitted together and sealed with tar. We cut a window in the top one and put in a translucent slab of mica. It wasn't great, but at least we'd have half a notion what was outside. We braced the boats with timbers so they couldn't be crushed inward. It looked good. So why were my knees feeling like cooked noodles? Maybe it was that I still hadn't figured out what to do about the zombies.

We had the submersible boat ready in time for the next whirlpool. The upper boat was fastened in place with hinges on one side and removable ties on the other. It was crude but it would do. We had a small supply of food; we did not expect to be away long.

Sinbad gave orders for the ship to wait upon our return. If we didn't appear within a week, then it should sail to the home port for some other mission. Then the three of us climbed in, sat on the seats, shipped the oars, swung down the upper boat, and tied it in place. It was dark inside, but some wan light filtered in through the window. A hoist on the Fat Chance lowered us into the water with a splash. We were on our way.

Sinbad and I took the oars and rowed, guiding the craft toward the forming whirlpool. Once that current caught us we relaxed, physically; it would do the rest.

"I'm thinking this is not a good idea," Sinbad said.

Duban and I both laughed, treating it as a joke, and thus it became one. It was of course too late to change our minds. Nevertheless, thoughts of Jewel coursed through my mind, lying nude on the bed, invitingly. She had truly restored me to potency, and I loved her for it. Or maybe it was the other way around. Then my thoughts morphed into an image of my beloved first wife. Perhaps I was about to join her in death.

The current caught us. We shipped the oars again and touched up the tar seal. So far no water was leaking in, but we were still floating high enough so that there was only splashing. I felt the craft accelerating as the current carried it around the circuit.

Duban peered through the mica window. "We're getting there," he reported.

"We never would have known," Sinbad muttered with sour irony. If I hadn't known better I might have thought he was looking a bit seasick himself. Probably it was a trick of the shadow.

Then he retched. Fortunately he managed to hold it in. We certainly didn't need the smell of vomit in our close confinement.

Now the craft accelerated. "Sit down, hold on," I told Duban. He was happy to obey.

"Oh, you're going to get it now, master." It was Faddy, of course, reveling in our discomfort.

"You are referring to the ambergris, of course," I told him.

"That too," he agreed with a sinister smile. "Wait until you meet the maidens."

He was obviously teasing us. I did not deign to rise to the bait.

The craft swung around in an ever-tighter circle, moving at incredible velocity. I closed my eyes and hung on. Was the contraption sturdy enough? Or would it fly apart and cast us into the rushing water?

Then we were at the center, spinning madly. That continued for a brief eternity. Then, abruptly, it ceased.

"And we are there," Faddy announced. "Good luck with the zombies, master." He faded out.

We pried open the craft. Light washed in. We were grounded on a beach. It looked almost pleasant. Palm trees lined its inner edge.

"Where's the ambergris?" Sinbad asked.

We got out and looked around. There was no sign of ambergris, or anything else. The beach was clear.

Then there was a cry. "Men!"

We whirled. There, passing the palms, were women, dozens of them, each more nude and shapely than the others. They were charging toward us, their flesh bouncing in fascinating ways.

Before we could properly react, they were upon us. One flung her arms around me and put her face to mine. She sought to kiss me. That was when I realized that she had no face. Her head was a blob of what seemed like solidified cloud stuff, shaped about right, but with only sockets for the eyes and a mound for the nose. Her hair consisted of streamers of vapor. Her body was similar, with mounds in the right places and shapely thighs, but all white cloud.

Whatever she was, she was not exactly human.

Now I'm not particularly prejudiced, particularly when it comes to bare women. But this was not my style. "Get away from me," I said.

"No, no, I love you!" she responded, the words issuing from the vent that was her mouth. She pressed her pelvis against me. Trying to push her away, I moved my hands across her back and found her bottom. It felt interesting, but it was more cloud stuff. I suspected it would be possible to, well, penetrate her, as a man does a woman, but inside her would merely be more cloud.

Assuming I would be potent with her regardless, which was highly dubious. So it was easy for me to do the right thing. "I am a married man. I will not tarry with the likes of you. Now give over, hussy, before I treat you unkindly."

"No no, I love you!" she repeated. It seemed that her head was filled with cloud stuff also.

I tried to pull her arms off me, but where I gripped her turned to vapor and I had no purchase. So I walked to the edge of the sea, and into it. Soon I was waist deep.

As I thought, her cloud stuff couldn't handle water. It floated, separating her substance from me. Her arms still clung, but I ducked down below the surface, and was free.

I came up and looked around. Sinbad and Duban were still entangled in cloud stuff. "Get in the water!" I called.

They heard me and lurched into the sea, carrying cloud maidens with them. In moments they too were wet but free. The ghostly girls stood at the edge, frustrated.

"That was interesting," Sinbad said. "In other circumstances I might like to learn more of clouds."

"It was appalling," Duban said. "She was all over me."

I exchanged a glance with Sinbad, and did not argue the case. It would not be long before the boy got interested in shapely bare female figures. No need to rush him.

"I think there is nothing here for us," I said. "Let's get back in the boat and row to the other island." Because now I saw a nearby isle, and it looked as though the carcass of a whale was there. We had merely landed on the wrong one.

We hauled the boat off the beach and clambered in, straight-arming affectionate maidens. Dunking made them let go without otherwise hurting them. They weren't afraid of the water; they simply couldn't handle it. We were soaked but otherwise unharmed.

We oriented on the other island, and were delighted to see that the massive lump on the beach *was* a whale; as we approached, the stink of it smote my nostrils.

"Ooops," Sinbad said. "The walking dead."

Now I saw them, coming from the nearby palms. Dozens of zombies, with rotting flesh galore. They had spied us with their deteriorating eyeballs. They looked hungry. They did not venture into the water; evidently that was impassible for them, as it was for the cloud maidens.

"I could be wrong," Duban said. "But I don't think they're going to let us search for ambergris unscathed."

Sinbad shuddered. "They want a piece of us, just as the cloud maidens do. Just not the same piece."

I got an idea. "A causeway!" I exclaimed.

Sinbad and Duban looked at me.

"We can make a causeway by dredging sand from the shallow sea floor," I said. "A ramp between the isles."

Duban caught on first. He was a smart boy. "The maidens will cross!"

Then Sinbad did. "And seek to make love to the zombies."

"And will not be dissuaded," I concluded. "While we, ignored, fetch and load the ambergris."

The others nodded. We now had a feasible plan of attack. Assuming that nothing went wrong.

CHAPTER SIX

"One problem," said Sinbad. "How do we build the causeway?"

I bit my lip, perhaps harder than I intended. With a taste of salty blood filling my mouth, I realized that my plan was brilliant...if we had the proper time.

As I thought about this, hard, I was more than aware of the walking dead approaching. Where did they come from? And where, exactly, were we? My best guess was a spirit realm. I had heard a mystic once discuss parallel realms that overlapped our own. A fascinating concept, but one that hurt my head. The whirlpool had brought us down to the nether regions, wherever this was, where the dead walked again, and fair maidens were nothing but exciting puffs of cloud-like shapes.

"Father, if I may," said Duban, his little face looking nervously from me to the approaching corpses, some of which clawed their way toward us on nothing more than hands, their legs long since gone. A horrific sight if I had ever seen one. To the boy's credit, he handled it all with a calm that I certainly wasn't feeling.

"Out with it, boy," I said.

"I can handle this," he said. "I'm sure of it. My control over the elements is strengthening."

I thought about it, even as the walking dead continued pouring through the shrubs and trees, bearing down on us inevitably. On the far isle, I could see the fair, cloud-like maidens watching all of this with obvious interest. How often did sailors end up on these shores? And how did the undead know of our arrival? What had alerted them?

The stink of the whale filled my nostrils, so strong that bile rose up in the back of my throat. Another stink soon mixed with that of the massive beast: the undead, their rotting flesh, soil and decaying garments wafting to us so strong that this time I did turn and wretch.

The ambergris was here, waiting. All we needed was time.

And now the first of the undead was upon Sinbad. I drew my own scimitar, but Sinbad was faster. His own flashed brilliantly, catching whatever was the source of light in these dull skies, and promptly hacked off the foul creature's rotting head. It landed in the sand, its jaw still napping. Headless, the creature lumbered past us, stumbling in the lapping currents, and then finally pitching forward.

I realized that a convergence of corpses, with a taste for human brain, qualified as an emergency to use magic, even though it galled me to think I had given in so quickly.

"Fine," I said. "But be quick about it."

Duban grinned, and as more and more of the walking dead approached, my son, who had been prophesied to be a powerful wizard, so powerful that greatest wizard in Djinnland had conspired to destroy him at a young age, stepped forward and raised his hands. The sand around him erupted in hundreds of dervishes, swirling around the undead, clearly disorientating them.

Duban, who had closed his eyes, opened them now and grinned. He was truly a powerful young wizard. He kept one hand up, and with his other he motioned toward the narrow channel that separated the two islands. A great wind appeared to erupt, although I felt no such wind. The water, clearly agitated, began lapping and churning...and parting.

Amazingly, the young man cleared a path through the water, revealing dry land, and now the waif-like puffs of nubile female figures crossed rapidly, seeing their opening. They disappeared behind the haze of churning sand, and as my stepson stood there, holding at bay both the elements, Sinbad slapped my shoulder hard, jarring me into action.

With the sounds of unnatural love making going on behind the storm of sand, mercifully blocking my son's view, Sinbad and I worked quickly.

It was messy work, indeed. We used our scimitars to gut the mighty creature, working our way towards its epic intestines. Once there we waded through muck and filth and slime, hacking and cutting, until we came upon the massive lumps of fetid ambergris, found deep within its stomach. To my shock, a great beak was embedded in one of the lumps…and I saw the practical use of ambergris for the great whale…to help ease such sharp, bony protrusions through its digestive tract.

Shortly, Sinbad and I had loaded the boat with our foul-smelling cargo, a cargo that was a treasure indeed, for it would be used later, once dried, as a valuable additive in perfumery. Some claimed it to be an aphrodisiac…which got me thinking.

But those thoughts were quickly quelled when a great, piercing screech erupted above the sounds of undead love making, churning sand, and rushing water.

I looked up, gasping. High above, was a massive bird. No, not just any bird. A giant roc, so enormous that it could easily crush our little submersible with its powerful talons. I stared, stunned. Will wonders never cease?

It circled once, then tucked its wings in and dived toward us.

CHAPTER SEVEN

Faddy appeared. "You mortals have a problem," he said with seeming satisfaction.

"If you're not going to help, smug ifrit, begone!" I snapped.

He sighed. "Very well, I will help. Consider the nature of rocs."

"They're big birds!" I said, frustrated.

But Sinbad caught on. "Despite their size, they're timid birds, fearful of sons of Adam, who they know have fearsome things like crossbows. We can scare it off." He jumped and waved his arms.

But the roc was still coming.

I got smart. "I bet it doesn't eat zombies. They're rotten, and they bite."

"Or cloud maidens," Duban said. "They have no real flesh."

Then the roc was upon us, talons extended, its huge beak gaping wide. I whipped out my scimitar and sliced viciously at that beak.

The bird sheered off. In a moment it was past us and sailing back into the sky.

"I scared it off!" I exclaimed, gratified.

"Or it took me for a zombie," Sinbad said. Now I saw that he was holding up his tattered shirt, which did resemble zombie apparel.

"Or a cloud maiden," Duban said. He was standing with his hands inside his shirt, poking it out like a formidable bosom. He was small, beardless, and fair: obviously a maiden.

"So we used our wits and prevailed," I said. "Good job, all."

"You missed the point, dull mortals," Faddy said.

"Oh?" I said, annoyed. "And what was your point, brilliant immortal?"

"I told you to consider the nature of rocs. Where do they reside?"

Sinbad clapped a hand to his head. "By the Isle of Diamonds and Serpents! That's a far sail from here, our next stop. What would a roc want with zombies? It shouldn't be here."

"But it *is* here," I pointed out.

"Precisely," Faddy said, looking at me as if I were stupid. That's bad enough when Jewel does it, worse when my former slave does it. I'd hate to think it was justified. But I certainly didn't get his point.

"It's *not* here," Duban said, catching on. "It's an illusion. I wondered why there was no big downdraft of air as it passed. Because it had no substance."

"Smart lad," Faddy said approvingly.

"Posted here to scare away anyone who is not a zombie or cloud maiden," Sinbad said. "So that no one will steal the ambergris."

"Smart man," Faddy agreed.

"Who posted it here?" I asked. "Not the zombies or cloud maidens."

"There is the question," Faddy agreed, fading out.

Disconcerted, I changed the subject. "We have a return whirlpool to catch."

"Maybe first we should let the cloud maidens go home," Duban said. If I didn't know better, I might have thought that he was a bit taken with these affectionate female forms.

I looked at the zombies. Most were finally extricating themselves from the embraces of the maidens, who seemed to be tiring of getting rejected. Both groups were probably ready to go home.

The avenue between the isles had filled in with water once Duban ceased focusing on it. Now he whistled, getting the attention of the maidens, who evidently liked to be whistled at. "Go home!" he called, and made his gesture. The waters parted and the path resumed. The maidens hastily disengaged and ran across it, some of them waving at Duban, who waved back.

It occurred to me that the boy might be growing up sooner than we expected. He knew that there was no future with these maidens, but what about when he encountered real ones?

When the last maiden was across, Duban relaxed and the sea filled in again. The two isles were now safely separated.

Several cloud maidens stood at the verge and gestured imploringly to Duban. They had evidently figured him for an easier mark. It seemed that the cloud stuff in their heads was not entirely dense.

"Maybe I was too hasty," he said musingly. "They seem like nice folk."

"We have work to do," Sinbad said.

"We do," I agreed immediately. But I wondered exactly why the maidens were so eager to make it with mortal men. Could it be that they might thereby obtain a bit of mortal substance that would replace an equivalent amount of cloud stuff and take them a tiny step closer to the living state? Were a mortal man to remain with them long enough, the maidens might thus slowly approach mortality themselves. In that manner they would become ever more desirable.

If I ever got deposed as king and given the chance to choose my mode of execution, I might ask to be put in a sealed boat and fed into the whirlpool. My enemies would be sure that meant violent extinction. Instead I would settle down with Cloudia and in time make a real woman of her.

"Are you sure your mind is on our mission?" Sinbad asked.

"Now it is," I said regretfully.

We rowed the boat around Zombie Isle, searching for the whirlpool. The zombies saw us but couldn't reach us, as they did not venture into the water. So they trudged back the way they had come, which happened to be the same way we were going. On the far side of the isle we saw what had to be Zombie City, with decrepit buildings. Here there were zombie females— I would not go so far as to call them maidens, as they plainly had been roughly used and were by no means fresh—some of whom gestured to us the way the cloud maidens had.

"If I had to choose, I'd choose clouds," Sinbad said gruffly. I couldn't have said it better myself. The zombies would bite our heads off, literally. Not so, the cloud maidens. There were worse fates for a man than to be marooned among such creatures, as I had already concluded.

The tide was going out. Where could it go, but back to our own realm? We just might have solved the mystery of where the waters of the seas went, every day and every night. When the tide receded, all that water had to go *somewhere*. Not that anyone would believe us.

And there was the forming whirlpool. We rowed madly to intercept it. Then, as the outer swirl caught us, we shipped oars and battened down the hatch.

We were on our way back to the ship, mission accomplished. I hoped our other stops would be as easy.

CHAPTER EIGHT

When the spinning stopped and we were adrift again, we unhatched the upper half of our vessel and I promptly retched over the railing.

I had managed not to vomit going down, but coming up was far longer and rougher and the spinning had seemed endless. Even the great Sinbad, sailor extraordinaire, looked a little green. I was secretly pleased at this, knowing that my jealousy of the man was unwarranted.

We spotted our vessel rising and falling on the swells. As we each picked up an oar and headed toward it, I considered the source of my jealousy of the man. Was I not a king? Was I not married to perhaps the most beautiful woman in all the realm? Had I not previously been married to another rare beauty? Yes, to all of the above.

Ah, but I did not have a great reputation for adventures. Sure, I had recently had an epic quest that would rival anything Sinbad had *allegedly* done, but my adventures had yet to garner songs of praise or poems of worship.

Who needs it? I spat.

Running a kingdom was challenging enough. And was I not adding to my own adventurous legacy?

No, I thought. You are only adding to Sinbad's.

I sighed. Sometimes you just couldn't win.

I looked at Duban and felt gratified to spend time with this most unusual boy. He was not my on, not of my blood, but I felt a kinship to him that knew no bloodlines. My own son had been cruelly murdered, and after many years of mourning, Jewel and Duban had later filled the void.

Filled it and then some.

Where the last few years of my life I had been left wandering and alone, confused and lost, these past few months I had found myself again.

And yet…I still longed for adventure.

Perhaps I was not as famous as Sinbad, but I had something even greater: the love of a good woman, and the devotion of a boy with whom I could do no wrong.

As I rowed toward the rising and falling ship, I looked again at Sinbad, and saw the grim determination on his face. He cared not for his reputation or the women who swooned after him and his legendary exploits. He cared only for the one who was stolen from him. His own wife.

Quick-witted and fearless, already Sinbad had proven to be a capable companion. Admittedly, it was hard not to like the guy.

Camel dung.

Shortly, we were aboard, and the ambergris safely stored below decks, where it would continue its long process of transformation: from whale gunk to valuable treasure.

For our success, the captain poured us all a draught of excellent wine…and cool water for my son. As evening approached, the musical instruments appeared, and my son asked if we would mind so much if he played. In good spirits, I told him to show them how it was done. Duban grinned, grabbed the lyre, and soon struck up a merry tune, in which the other ramshackle musicians struggled to keep pace with. Sinbad, in rare good spirits—after all, we were now one step closer to rescuing his wife—leaped to his feet and kicked up his boots and stomped a traditional jig. He even grabbed the captain and spun the bearded man around like a lithe maiden. The crew, myself included, guffawed and clapped, and this was how we spent the next few hours of light.

Come morning, with my head feeling as if it had been cracked open and feasted upon by zombies, I climbed above deck to find Sinbad and the captain engaged in an urgent dialogue.

"Ho," I said, stepping over bodies still sprawled out from last night's drinking.

"How' goes it, Niddala?" said Sinbad, keeping to our public ruse.

"If I felt any worse," I said, "I would be dead."

Sinbad laughed heartily and slapped my back. "We are deciding our next course, Niddala, perhaps you would like to weigh in."

His words rubbed me the wrong way. No one asked the king if "perhaps" he would like to weigh in. Indeed, I was used to those waiting on baited breath for my directives.

But I wasn't the king. Not out here. Here, I was another sailor. Another adventurer. I thought about Sinbad's situation. "It seems to me," I said. "That the fastest way to redeem your wife is gather the greatest amount of riches. As valuable as ambergris is, it cannot replace that of diamonds and rubies and emeralds."

"And gold!" hissed the captain, slapping his hands together, and for the first time I caught a wicked glint in his eye, and my old instincts kicked in. Something told me that perhaps the hardened sailor might not be trustworthy.

"Yes," I said guardedly. "And gold."

"Hang on!" cried the captain, and he scurried past me and grabbed a young sailor by the shoulder. He hauled the buck-toothed lad over to us. "Tell him what you told me a fortnight ago, and be quick about it."

"Captain?"

The captain promptly clapped the youth behind his ear. "Out with it!"

The young man looked nervously from me to Sinbad, and then to the captain, and then he began his tale. Two weeks ago, while sailing on a vessel similar to this, he had heard singing. Beautiful singing that made him weep. The singing had reached his ears from the fog-filled night, clear and sharp and so hauntingly beautiful that he had felt love for the first time in his short, bitter life. The youth had dashed over to the wheel, where he had fought with the captain, begging the man to turn the vessel around. But the captain had been savvy and had known of the enchanted singing. He had plugged his ears with cotton and wax, blocking out the enchanted Siren calls, whose beautiful voices made it all but impossible to turn back away from rocks hidden just below the surface. The boy, who had been so possessed by the Siren's song, had to be chained below decks to keep him away from the steering helm.

"A strange story indeed, but what does this have to do with our mission," I asked the captain.

But Sinbad was already nodding. "The Sirens guard a grand treasure. Some claim the biggest treasure of all."

"I do not understand. If they guard a treasure, then why sing about it?"

"Because their voices are a trap," said the lad. "Never have I heard such beauty. Never. I weep at night when I think of them—"

The captain clapped the boy again, so hard he stumbled forward. "Oh give it a rest, lad."

"They were lucky to escape," said Sinbad. "Most ships would have been destroyed against the rocks, and the treasure would have been safe." He looked at the boy. "Your captain was indeed a savvy man. He saved his ship and your life." He turned to the boy. "And you know where this region of the sea is located?"

The boy nodded dreamily. "It is forever seared into my memory, Sinbad."

"Good, then you will lead us back?"

"And my ship?" said the captain.

Sinbad looked at me, then at the captain. "Let us worry about your ship."

CHAPTER NINE

The captain did not look entirely sanguine about that, but since we had hired his ship and he would get a share of what wealth we garnered, he did not object.

Actually I was not sanguine either. Those Sirens were evidently dangerous. We needed to plan carefully, or our ambergris would merely be added to their treasure, and we would be literally sunk.

We set sail for Siren Island. I steeped myself with ginger glop to stifle my sickness and got together privately with Sinbad and Duban. "How do we deal with the Sirens?"

"We plug our ears, of course," Sinbad said confidently.

I glanced at Duban, encouraging him to weigh in. He did. "Plugging our ears may save the ship, but then how can we get the sirens' treasure? Surely it is well hidden, and only they know where."

"Excellent question," I said. "Do we have an answer?" I glanced significantly at Sinbad.

"I hadn't thought of that," the man admitted, to my satisfaction. He might be a great adventurer, but he had missed the obvious. Of course I had missed it too, but had played the scene well. "One of us will have to listen."

"And be ensorceled by the sound, as that young sailor was? That one won't be much help to the others."

"Maybe I can help," Duban said. "I like music and appreciate its power. Music and magic interconnect strongly. I think I can devise a spell that will make us immune to the lure. That is, we can hear it, but won't be overcome."

"Brilliant," Sinbad agreed. "We can anchor the ship beyond the Sirens' range and go in on a small boat to negotiate."

"Negotiate?" I asked skeptically. "What with? All they want is to wreck our ship and take whatever it has. All we want is their treasure, surely composed of all the treasures of all the ships they have lured, wrecked, and pillaged before. This isn't a dialog between friends; this is war."

"Ah, but if we are immune to their devastating song," Sinbad said cannily, "then we will be in a position to kill them and take their treasure regardless."

"Assuming we can find it," I said sourly.

"Then we can negotiate after all," Duban said. "We will threaten to kill all of them, but will spare any who lead us to their treasure."

Sinbad nodded. "You will make a fine king, in due course. You have the essence."

Duban did not respond, but I knew he was stifling a retort that he never intended to be any kind of king. But he would have years to change his mind.

"Then let's get to the magic," I said. "But let's also keep it to ourselves. I don't trust that captain."

Both Sinbad and Duban nodded. They had picked up on the captain's shifty look.

"This spell will make us tone deaf for several days," Duban said. "Until it wears off." Then he played some eerie music on the lyre. At first it was lovely, then it went flat, losing its appeal. Had the boy lost his touch? Then I realized that his fingers were still plucking the strings, but all the notes had become the same. Or rather, we heard them as all the same. We had become tone deaf.

Then I became aware of something else. I no longer felt queasy. My sea sickness had abated. Somehow the spell had changed that too. I understood from somewhere that something in the ears related to balance and thus to sea sickness, so changing what they heard must have done it.

We sailed on, and in three days my sickness returned. I could hear music again. "Um, Duban—" I said.

He smiled. "Gladly, Father." He played the theme again, and my queasiness abated.

"Thank you, son." I was really getting to like that boy.

In due course we approached the area the sailor had told us about. "Soon we'll hear the Siren song," he said eagerly. "I can almost hear it now." He cocked his head.

"Drop anchor!" Sinbad told the captain.

"But we're still just out of range," the sailor protested.

"Precisely," Sinbad said.

The three of us huddled privately so that Duban could give us a good dose of magic music. I knew it was effective because my seasickness was gone. We rehearsed our strategy for dealing with the Sirens one last time. Then we made sure of our weapons and went to our rowboat. Sinbad directed the captain to remain here until we returned, as before.

"Wait!" the young sailor cried. "I want to go too!"

"Camel dung!" Sinbad muttered. "He'll be a nuisance."

"I can lead you right to them!" the man insisted. "Otherwise you could cast about for hours looking!"

"We'll follow the song," Sinbad said.

But I caught his eye: we could no longer hear the song as such. The others didn't know that, but we could indeed cast about blindly.

Sinbad decided to be magnanimous. "Very well, sailor, you may come. But I will not be responsible for the likely doom you are bringing on yourself."

"Oh thank you, sir!" the sailor cried, jumping into the boat. I made a mental note: the Siren song lured men even when they knew it could kill them.

"Make yourself useful," Sinbad said. "Take an oar."

The sailor gladly agreed. Soon the sailor and I were rowing, while Sinbad and Duban faced the other way, peering into the forming mists.

"You're in for something special," a voice murmured in my ear. It was the ifrit Faddy. "Those fishfolk are something to behold. But don't trust them farther than you can kiss them."

"Thanks for the advice," I said. But I felt to make sure I had the magic lamp on me, just in case we needed to be bailed out. Lamprey still served me, though I never called him unless the need was dire.

"I hear them!" the sailor said as he rowed. "Don't you?"

"Of course we do," Sinbad said gruffly. "But we are resisting the lure."

The truth was all we heard was a monotonous ululation. I realized that the sailor was proving to be more useful than we had thought, because the Sirens would assume that all of us were as fascinated as he was. But I wondered: just what did the Sirens *do* with the men of the ships that wrecked? Because as far as I knew, no sailor had ever returned from any ship caught by the Sirens. I was glad I had my scimitar handy.

The ululation increased in intensity. It sounded like nothing so much as dismal wailing. This caused captains to wreck their ships?

"I'm coming!" the sailor said. "I love you!"

I was almost sorry I couldn't hear the tune. It must be quite compelling. "Remember," I said. "Our best bet is to treat them with contempt. Get them riled so they don't think straight."

Then a head appeared by the boat. We saw the lovely face and bosom of a swimming mermaid. The sailor and I stopped rowing. We were evidently there.

"Here to meee," the Siren sang.

The sailor leaped out of the boat to join her. So much for contempt. She threw her arms about him, kissed him, and drew him under the surface of the sea. Just like that they were gone.

"Did I mention how we appreciate your magic?" I asked Duban.

He didn't answer. He was staring at the next mermaid. She was a truly luscious creature, with flowing blond hair, a face like the fabled Helen of Troy, and a torso that wavered tantalizingly in the ripples of the water. "Come to meeee," she sang to him.

"I think not," Duban said. "But you certainly are pretty."

Pretty? That was the understatement of the year.

The mermaid frowned, as well she might. She did not realize that both Duban's magic and his youth prevented him from being instantly enraptured by her voice and aspect. "Not?"

I interposed. "We are here to negotiate, fishtail."

She looked at me, plainly annoyed. "Why are you not already in the water seeking my embrace?"

"Well, we don't care to get wet. Why don't you come aboard and we'll talk."

Her mouth worked for a moment without making a sound. She simply did not know what to make of this impudence.

More Sirens appeared around the boat. "Come to meee," they chorused.

"We have come to negotiate with the Sirens," Sinbad said. "But a Siren is part woman and part bird. You look like routine mermaids to me. We'll not join you."

The creatures exchanged frustrated glances. Then their evident leader spoke. She was a black haired beauty whose imposing breasts needed no song enhancement to make them fascinating. "There are different species of Sirens. We are sea dwellers. Why are you not hopelessly fascinated by our song?"

"I'm sure it's a nice song," I said in the manner of an adult complimenting a child. "But my son Duban plays a better melody on the lyre." I frowned. "Now let's get down to business. We are here to take your treasure. We will spare any who lead us to it. The others we will slay." I touched the hilt of my scimitar.

The head Siren swelled up until her bosom threatened to float right out of the water. "We will overturn your boat, dump you in the water, and drown you, you disreputable oaf!"

I made a beckoning gesture. "Welcome to try, honey. We'll lop the arms off any who try to grab this boat. Now are you going to come here and sit your pert posterior on my lap, so we can talk while I fondle your doubtlessly adequate body?"

I thought she was going to rise the rest of the way out of the water, so steamed was her expression. Then she changed her approach. "Perhaps that would be nice." She put her arms up to me so that I could catch hold and draw her up onto me.

I hesitated. Would she really do it, or was this a ploy to try to kill me?

One way to find out. I knew Sinbad and Duban were on guard. I caught her arms and lifted her. She wriggled her tail to boost herself, and flopped up against me. As her tail left the water it shimmered and shifted, becoming a truly fine pair of legs. Indeed, her body was marvelously fit throughout. Gloriously nude, she sat on my lap. She wasn't even wet. She brought her face close to mine, puckered for a kiss.

"You do realize, of course," I said calmly, "that if you try to bite me I will promptly cut your silly head off?"

"I realize," she said, and delivered a wonderfully sweet kiss. "Now shall we talk before or after I seduce you?"

For perhaps the first time in my life, I was glad for my impotence with strange women. It had become a secret weapon. "Before."

"Before," she agreed. "Now what's this about your taking our treasure?"

Now our dialogue should get interesting.

CHAPTER TEN

D uban was looking at me with darkened eyes.
I didn't need to be a seer to know what he was thinking: he didn't approve of me cavorting with any woman other than his mother. And, quite, frankly, he probably didn't approve of me cavorting with his mother either. If I wasn't careful, my negotiating skills might be misconstrued as something less than honorable. Although I was a sovereign king and had access to concubines and mistresses, and fathers veritably shoved their daughters onto me, I had had no such interest in pursuing such dalliances. Jewel was truly the woman for me, not to mention the only woman who awakened a passion that had lain dormant for so many years. For that I was grateful... and faithful.

Truly, I loved Jewel, and I loved our physical relationship. I would not want to lose that under any circumstances.

All of which led me to physically remove the buxom young Siren from my lap. Her curves were soft and her flesh taut and any other man on earth would have been tempted beyond reason.

The Siren was clearly not used to this. "Have I fallen already out of favor?" she asked, pouting.

I caught Duban's approving gaze. How much access the powerful young man had to my thoughts, I did not know, but he surely knew the depth of my love for his mother.

"Of course not," I said. "I was finding negotiation, ah, difficult with such a fine creature sitting on my lap."

She nodded, approving of my response. That she was sitting nude in front of two men and a half, she cared not. With each breath, her large breasts reflected the setting sun in ways that I would never, ever forget.

"So tell me, handsome mortal, how are you not affected by our beautiful voices? This has never happened before."

I opened my mouth to speak but Sinbad jumped in. "We are tone deaf, fair maiden."

"Tone deaf? What does this mean?"

"It means your music is lost on us," I said.

She looked carefully at each of us, lingering longer on Duban. Her eyes narrowed slightly, as did his. I wondered if a psychic connection had been made, of the sort I was not privy to.

"And all of you suffer from this unfortunate malady?" she asked.

"Yes," I said irritably. Her perfect flesh was damn distracting and we had a treasure to find, not to mention Duban's spell would be wearing off soon. "Now where is—"

"And this has nothing to do with this intriguing young man?" she asked leaning forward, studying Duban.

"Nonsense," I said, gripping my scimitar. To end such a lovely creature's life was a crime, until I realized that her beauty could all be an illusion. Or not. Either way, I would not die out here, on this simple boat, at the hands of psychotic immortal vixens.

She leaned back again, although her gaze lingered on Duban. "A most unusual young man."

"Enough," I said, raising my voice and pointing my sword. "Now take us to your treasure our lose your beautiful head."

"Nonsense," she said, "you will not harm me."

"Why wouldn't I harm you?" I asked, blinking.

"You need me to take you to our treasure."

"There are others here who will take me, or they will all be slain—"

"And if they are all slain, then who will take you?"

"I am certain one or two will wish to be spared?"

"And if not, mortal? What if they choose to follow their leader in death?"

"You are their leader?" I asked.

She turned her full gaze onto me and I swallowed hard. By Allah, she was a beautiful woman. Duban was looking at me again, and I focused my thoughts.

"Of course," she said. "As I have been for eons."

"Then you have certainly led many a sailor to his death."

She returned her gaze to me. Something close to pleasure crossed her fine features. "Oh, not all deaths have been catastrophic."

"What does that mean?"

She grinned again and now Faddy appeared next to me, invisible to everyone but me. And perhaps Duban. I truly did not know the extent of the boy's considerable power. "They're using our young sailor as a sex slave, master."

I merely nodded, not risking speaking, or even sub-vocalizing. I also did not know the extent of the Siren's powers.

Faddy continued. "He's being used over and over, draining him of fluid and life. He will be dead soon."

I could not imagine a better way to go. But I had other problems to focus on. Primarily, our leverage seemed to have been nullified. If the Sirens would risk death rather than forfeit their vast treasure, I had to use another angle.

"What use is the treasure to you, Sea Hag?" I said.

"It is beautiful to look at."

"And you would risk your life…immortality, before giving up beauty?"

"Perhaps, but you would be foolish to find out first hand."

We were getting nowhere. "Out with it, Sea Hag. What is that you want?"

She looked at me coolly, her features beautiful and timeless. Her age was nearly impossible to gauge. Then she looked from me to Duban. "The boy."

I stiffened. "What about the boy?"

"I want him. He seems…amusing."

"Never—"

"It is okay, Niddala," said Duban calmly. "They can have me if they so desire."

"Never!"

And that's when I felt a calming presence surround me. Months ago, I had experienced powerful telepathy. This feeling was similar, as if someone had nestled close to me. So close that they were, in fact, in my mind. Duban, as far as I was aware, did not have such abilities. Still, he was able to radiate a *feeling* towards me. A peaceful feeling. I glanced at him sharply and he smiled serenely and the feeling intensified.

Duban might be young in years but he was wise for his age. For any age. He was letting me know that everything was okay, that perhaps he even had a plan.

"Camel dung," I mumbled under my breath. "Fine. You may have the boy."

"My lord—er, Nidalla, are you sure?" asked Sinbad, grabbing my arm.

I looked again at Duban and he nodded once. "Yes," I said weakly, although never had I felt less sure about anything. "I'm sure."

The wicked sea creature leaped from the boat. "Then come! The water is fine." She cackled with laughter. "Your treasure awaits. Follow me."

"But we cannot follow you into the ocean, Sea Witch," I hissed.

"Oh, it is not very deep at all, mortal. Follow me if you dare. And don't forget the boy."

She grinned again, revealing long, curved teeth that I had not seen before. She turned, flashed her backside, and disappeared beneath the waves.

CHAPTER ELEVEN

hat the Hades.

We hastily stripped off our clothing and dived after her, stroking on the surface. Duban and I weren't great swimmers, being landlubbers, but Sinbad was fair. She showed up before us, a far better swimmer than we were, and she wasn't even using her tail. She was swimming right in front of me and I could see her legs flashing together and apart.

The she-dog! She was deliberately vamping us with her nether flesh. "Remember the boy!" I called to her angrily.

"Ooops," she agreed ruefully, and her tail reformed. Had she really forgotten? I did not fully trust the nature of her interest in Duban. "Now down." Her flukes flashed as she dived.

We pursued her as well as we were able. Not far below the surface was the entrance to an underwater cave in the bank leading to an island. We followed her into it. Inside it angled upward and there was air. That was a relief; I could not hold my breath long.

And what a cave it was! I had seen geodes in my treasury, stones cracked open to reveal colorful crystals inside. This entire cave was a huge geode with highly reflective facets. A beam of sunlight angled down through a hole above, and the crystals coruscated where it struck, reflecting a range of colors from the glassy prisms. It was absolutely beautiful, and surely precious beyond description.

"Don't dawdle," the Siren chided us. "This is merely the entryway. Onward." Her flukes flashed again as she dived.

We followed, this time going deeper to a hole in the cave floor, trusting that this too led to a chamber with air. It did, though this one was darker. There was a muted glow from the walls, as of illuminated plants, so that we could see, but that was all. The other sirens were already here, ranged alongside their mistress. We would have trouble fighting them off, if it came to that, because we had foolishly left our weapons in the boat.

When we reached the bank there was another surprise. This chamber was huge, and filled to bursting with gold, silver, diamonds, rubies, emeralds, pearls, and works of art: carved jade statuettes, teak and mahogany reliefs, intricate sandalwood boxes, ivory figurines, and ornate alabaster lamps. Even bottles of rare wines, and papyrus scrolls that were surely rarer books. The treasures of countless wrecked ships. A tiny fraction of it would fill the hold of the Fat Chance and make the ship sluggish in the water from the weight.

"What do you think?" the Siren asked with a toothy smile as we clambered onto the dry cave floor.

Duban caught on first. "Your cave is full! You need to clear some of it out to have room for more valuable items hereafter."

"Exactly," she agreed. "We will give you one shipload for your mission, and on your return, if you wish, another shipload for your merchants. It will be a profitable venture for all concerned."

"What do you know of our venture?" Sinbad asked suspiciously.

"As much as we care to, Sinbad. It is a noble thing you attempt."

"You know my name!"

"And the names of your companions, King Aladdin and Magician Duban. Welcome to our humble abode."

We stared at her. "How—?" I asked.

"Word gets around. We track all ships of the region, so as to know what they contain. Yours is hardly worth harvesting, just some immature ambergris, and we already have more than enough of that. So we left it alone."

"You saw us coming!" Sinbad said.

"Literally and figuratively," she agreed.

"Then why—?"

"We wanted the boy, so we let you bring him to us. Why else? It isn't as though we need more stud service, not that Aladdin can provide that anyway."

The vixen knew too much. "Then why?" I echoed Sinbad, embarrassed.

"Why threaten to seduce you? It's a challenge. Ordinary sailors are no challenge at all, but you are. It would be fun to prove that the queen is not unique in that respect."

Way too much!

"You want me for what?" Duban asked grimly. He now seemed less certain that all was well.

She laughed. "Not that. We have no need to prey on the young. It is your potent magic we want."

"My magic is not for the likes of you."

She gave him a steady gaze. "Are you sure?"

And, surprisingly, Duban backed down. "No."

"You have a notion what we want," the Siren continued. "You know that the deal we proffer is fair. That's why you agreed to come here."

"That is not the whole of it," Duban said tightly.

"Then it is time to present the whole of it. Duban, we are strong in our domain, but there are potential enemies who are stronger. We face serious mischief that we will be powerless to prevent. We don't know when or what, just that the danger lurks. But with a magician of your caliber on our side, we can perhaps fend it off. So we want an alliance with you. Since you will not betray your father, we must make an alliance with him too."

"An alliance!" I exclaimed. "Why should I want to have anything to do with you?"

"Because you are sailing into a deadly trap, Aladdin. We can help you. But we want a fair exchange."

I had received similar warnings before. "A shipload of treasure won't help me much if I die in a trap."

"Exactly," the Siren agreed. "The treasure is merely a pretext. We are trading that for the alliance with Duban. We are trading information for the alliance with you."

"What trap?" I demanded.

"We do not know the details of it, only that it relates to the woman, Sinbad's wife. When you ransom her, it will spring. You must be prepared or you are lost. You may be lost anyway." She turned to face Sinbad. "Your safest course is to give up your quest. We can provide you with a woman as lovely and obliging as your wife, if you wish."

"Never!" Sinbad said.

"Precisely. We do value loyalty." She turned back to Duban. "Do we have a deal?"

Duban nodded. "I will help you to the extent I can, when you need it. How will I know when that is?"

"Sylvie will accompany you." The Siren gestured, and one of the other mermaids swam forward, slender yet voluptuous as they all were.

"I don't want a girl with me!"

The Siren smiled. "Be not concerned. She will make an oath not to seduce you for three years. Then she will negotiate with Myrrh for an extension if you still don't want a concubine. You will not be molested."

Duban was obviously set back. "But to have such a creature with me—others will misunderstand."

"Not if she accompanies you in the form of a silver ring on your finger."

"You can do transformations?"

"Not of that magnitude; tail to legs is about our limit. But you can. All you need is guidance."

"Guidance?"

"Approach him, Sylvie," the Siren said. The mermaid did. "Take her hand, Duban." Duban reluctantly did. "Now concentrate of the image of the ring, Duban. Make her change, stage by stage. Be guided by the protocol in my mind." She knew Duban could read her mind, and was using that.

And, slowly, the mermaid changed form, first bending forward to catch her own toes with her free hand, forming a large ring in the water, part of which touched Duban's hand. Then it became smaller, until at last it was ring sized, and nestled securely on his left little finger.

"Free her to swim once a day, for her health," the siren said. "Otherwise she will be no trouble to you. You will be able to commune with her mentally, as you are in close contact, and if we need you, we will signal her."

Duban stared at what he had wrought, fascinated. A silvery ring on his finger, that I now saw had faint contours of a curled woman. Sylvie. The Siren had known how to direct Duban in using his formidable magic for this purpose. In the process she had amplified his power by showing him how it could be directed. She must have learned such tricks in the course of her centuries of life.

I exchanged a glance with Sinbad. We both knew that we would be better off allied with the Sirens than opposed to them. We did not want them as enemies.

Still, there were questions. "If you were this savvy about our nature and motives, why did you bother with the business in the boat?"

The Siren smiled. "We do enjoy a little flirtation on occasion."

"Flirtation! I threatened to cut off your head!"

"But you didn't mean it, any more than we meant to drown you. We simply had roles to play, until we could get private. The very fish have ears, out there."

I elected not to argue the case. For one thing, I feared she was smarter than I. Truly savvy women make me nervous.

"The young sailor," Sinbad said. "You took him."

I nodded. How would she explain away that evidence of bad intention?

"You may have him back, if he wants to rejoin you. Observe." The Siren touched a wall of the cave and a porthole opened.

Sinbad and I peered through it; Duban remained distracted by the ring. There was the sailor embracing a siren so closely it was hard to be sure whether she was wearing legs or tail. He was madly kissing her, and that was surely only the aspect that showed. Several other sirens were waiting nearby.

"Sailor!" Sinbad called. "We are about to return to the ship. Are you coming?"

"In a moment!" he gasped. Then he paused. "Oh, the ship. No, I'm happy here."

"You're wearing yourself out," Sinbad said. "It's not healthy."

"They've got pep pills. I can keep going indefinitely." Indeed, he finished with the one mermaid, who rolled out from under him, and another took her place. He clasped her, though he was starting to look gaunt.

It was apparent that the sailor was in his kind of heaven and did not want to give it up even for a moment, though he destroy himself. He was drugged on performance.

I sighed. We needed to get out of here before the tone deaf magic wore off, so that we did not get similarly overcome. "We have a deal," I said shortly.

"Wonderful." The Siren came and kissed me with such finesse that I did have to wonder whether she would be able to seduce me if given time. I suspected she could, despite my awareness that she was far, far older than she looked.

"Time to go," Sinbad said.

It was more than time.

CHAPTER TWELVE

The three of us were then given free rein of the underwater cavern, told to hand-pick our treasures. Sinbad, in dire need of a hefty payment to negotiate for his wife, picked out the most valuable jewels and gold coins. He bypassed silver entirely. Duban had an eye for mystical relics: a fabulous crystal ball, golden idols and chunky jewelry that veritably screamed enchantment. All of which he scooped up with glee, and I suspected that a ship or two transporting powerful wizards had met their end on these very rocks.

How many lives had the Sirens ended? I didn't know, but I figured in the hundreds, if not thousands. What possessed them? What drove them? Was it all for the valuable cargo? Cargo they had no use of other than to bask in its beauty?

I hadn't a clue, but I knew we needed to be moving. I wasn't sure how much longer Duban's spell would keep the Sirens' singing at bay. Indeed, I could hear their singing constantly in the background. Although many were here with us in the caverns, I suspected a few were always on the rock, singing, luring, destroying, killing.

I shook my head as I went through the treasure, picking out what I thought Jewel would like, and relics that would look nice in my palace. I felt like a woman out shopping in the market with her sisters. Except in this case, the market consisted of only treasure, and my "sisters" were none other than Sinbad and a powerful young wizard, who only seemed to be getting more powerful by the minute.

I picked out some portraits that were breathtaking, and jewel-encrusted bowls, goblets and something that could have been a wand. I'd probably give that to Duban. As I pointed to items, beautiful maidens collected them and deposited them in clear containers that I, for the life of me, could not fathom their composition. It appeared to be glass, but very fine and lightweight. Perhaps it was an enchanted material, known only to these vile vixens.

Sinbad's treasure of gold and jewels filled the majority of the boxes, which was fine. My kingdom was thriving and I, like the Sirens, had little use for gold and jewels, other to look at.

Perhaps I am not much different than the vixens, I thought, but then tossed the idea immediately. I did not make it a habit to lure and destroy and plunder.

"And how do we get this treasure to the ship?" I asked the beautiful leader, who was watching all of this from a high rock. I noted the perch gave her a view of the entire cavern, from where she could indeed sit and admire her priceless collection.

"We will take it out to you, of course. We have done this sort of thing before, although in reverse." She cackled at her own wicked joke.

As we were preparing to set out again, something else caught my eye. A rug, rolled tightly and leaning against the cave wall. A loose thread was blowing in the wind...except there was no wind down here. Having already owned such a magic carpet, I suspected what this was immediately. I pointed to it, and it, too, was added to our valuable cargo.

With our treasure selected, we were led out of the cavern the same way we had come. Duban, I noted, appeared relaxed and comfortable during the entire swim, while Sinbad and I swam with panicked desperation. And with my lungs near to bursting, we broke the surface of the ocean, near our simple rowboat, which had not strayed very far. The boy only smiled as Sinbad and I gasped, sucking great lungfuls of air.

Enchantment, I thought. *Wizards always have it easy.*

The next few hours were eventful as our horde of treasure, towed by a row of beautiful Sirens appeared next to the ship. The lads on board nearly fell into the water with them. They didn't need enchanted songs to lure them to their deaths. A healthy pair of floating breasts appeared to be all that was necessary.

There was a collective groan from the men, when the Sirens lifted their tails in unison, flashed the men, and dove under the surface. It was a good thing we were out of range of the cursed rock. No doubt the ship would have turned and followed right behind them.

With our treasure stowed aboard and the merchant vessel sitting low on the water, I knew we had reached its maximum capacity.

Later, Sinbad and I were sitting with the captain in his slightly less cramped quarters. Duban and the men were singing and dancing and stomping above deck, celebrating our epic haul of treasure.

Sinbad, I noted, appeared anxious.

He saw my concern and explained, "Every day that my wife is held captive is another day for her to be raped and tortured."

"Surely this is enough treasure to ransom your wife," I said.

At the mention of giving up the treasure, the ship captain looked stricken and a brief darkness clouded his features. He composed himself quickly. "It's enough to buy a small kingdom." And now the captain looked wistful, and I wondered what he had in mind.

"We can only see," said Sinbad. "But I think it's time to find out."

"And where is your wife being held captive?" I asked.

"Cloudland," said Sinbad grimly.

"I have never heard of this land," I said.

Sinbad smiled and I saw the old gleam of adventure return. "Because few have seen it, and fewer yet have returned."

"It seems," I said dryly, "that we have been hearing that a lot."

Sinbad chuckled lightly. "You are good luck, my King, as I suspected you would be. Anyone aided by such a powerful djinn must surely have luck on his side. In the past, my visits to the land of the dead or the caverns of the Sirens, would have ended very poorly for me. Sure, I might have come out of it alive, but my crew would have been long gone, and I might have suffered greatly. But with you here, yes, Allah is surely looking favorably upon us. So, indeed, few have seen these places, and fewer yet make it back alive, which is why I have high hope that we will survive yet again, and this time with my precious wife."

I was embarrassed by praise of luck, although a case could certainly be made for it. I prefer to think I lived by my wits and strength and cunning, but maybe my success was due to nothing more than good fortune and the grace of Allah.

I said, "Tell me more of this Cloudland."

"Ah, it needs to be seen to be believed," began Sinbad, and once again his dark eyes had that far-off look of a man who is forever restless, who forever craves adventures and a rolling deck beneath his feet.

Sinbad went on to describe Cloudland, a fantastical place that sat high in the clouds above an island a week's journey from here. The trees here grew to incomprehensible heights, reaching high into the clouds themselves. There a city was built, in the treetops, connected by precarious bridges and walkways, a city perpetually filled with roiling mist, thunderstorms and lighting. "Here, where the sun never shines, a great wizard lives."

"And this is where your wife is held captive?"

"Close," said Sinbad. "The great trees reach as high as the highest peak upon the mountain. It is within a cave, high above, and guarded by a serpent large enough to swallow two camels whole."

Duban turned green. I think my own heart might have fluttered. It was tempting to wish Sinbad luck and turn back with our treasure, but I had come to like the man, and his love for his wife was admirable. Not to mention, I did not want our hero's tale to say that King Aladdin fled at the first sign of insurmountable odds. Or seemingly insurmountable odds.

I nodded and clapped Sinbad heartily on his shoulder. "Then I suggest we set sail for Cloudland immediately."

The relief on his face was unmistakable. The frown on the captain's face was worrisome. In due course, we set sail for the isle of the giant trees.

And giant serpents, too, apparently.

CHAPTER THIRTEEN

"**D**on't sleep by day, master," Faddy told me. "It's not healthy."

"I'll do what I please, ifrit," I retorted. "Begone."

He went. That spook could really annoy me, because now he appeared when he chose, rather than when I chose. He was trying to direct my schedule?

The sea was calm, with moderate winds of the right direction: ideal sailing weather. After two days we were frankly bored. Duban kept me from being seasick by moderate doses of the tone-deaf spell, which I really appreciated. We played at dice for worthless pebbles, just for the diversion and to show Duban this aspect of male existence; all men gambled foolishly. We ate a good meal provided by the ship's galley, and drank a bit too much spiced sherbet. Sherbets required ice, and there was precious little of that aboard ship, because it didn't store well, so it was a special treat. Maybe the captain wasn't such a bad sort after all. Even Duban sampled the drink, learning another aspect of being a man, though I wouldn't let him over-indulge lest I had to answer to his mother. Really good drinks sometimes contained alcohol, which was of course forbidden to loyal followers of Allah. Naturally we pretended not to notice the tang. Then we slept.

I woke in darkness, which was odd because it had been midday when we napped. Then I realized that I was not in our cramped compartment, but in a boat. A closed boat. In fact it

63

was our double boat that we had used to ride the whirlpools. What was I doing here?

In a moment I felt around and found Sinbad and Duban on either side of me, both still sound asleep. This was really weird. How had we come here without waking?

"I told you, master. But you dismissed me unkindly."

For once I was glad to hear from Faddy. "I apologize for disrespecting you," I said contritely. "Now will you explain the situation?"

"Gladly, master. The wicked captain put bhang in your sherbet, such a dose that if an elephant sniffed it, it would sleep from week to week. Naturally you conked out. Then he hauled the three of you into the boats, closed them over you, and had his men lower you over the side to the water and cast you adrift. The men did not know the craft was occupied. They thought it was merely making room on the deck for future treasure."

My mind was slowly clearing. Bhang had never had great effect on me, which explained why I recovered first, though probably Faddy was exaggerating about the elephant. "This is a dastardly plot by the captain? I never did much like the look of the man."

"Even so, master. I tried to warn you."

"So you said," I agreed. Sometimes Faddy's communications lacked complete clarity, but this was not the time to argue that case. "So the captain is stranding us so he can abscond with the treasure?"

"Even so, master. No one else knows you are even gone. I think he means to take it all for himself and any henchmen who support him."

"Let's get the lid off," I said, sitting up and heaving at it. It swung up and the light of early afternoon poured in.

I looked around. There was no sign of the ship. With a fair wind it had obviously made good progress away from here, and we would never be able to catch it even if we were all in good rowing shape, which we weren't. There was no land either. We were stranded on the high seas, and for all the captain knew, would soon die of hunger and exposure here on the open water. It was one sinisterly neat ploy.

However, there were things the captain did not know about us, such as our identities, or my magic lamp, or Duban's growing ability as a magician. The crew knew him as as innocent young musician, that was all. We had resources, and this was not as serious a matter as it might have been.

I felt for the chest that held the Lamp. It wasn't there. Oops— it had been left behind, on the ship, as a thing of little value. Our situation had just become a notch more serious. But there still might be a remedy. "Faddy, would you care to zip off to the ship and fetch me the Lamp?"

"You're turning to that djinn instead of to me?" he demanded, offended.

I realized it would not be politic to point out that as ifrits went, Lamprey was like a mighty king compared to Faddy's lowly peasant, and could do proportionally more for me. "I have to," I said. "Lamprey remains bound to me. You don't. I freed you, remember?"

"Still," he said, only moderately mollified.

"But of course you *are* an ifrit, and surely could provide supernatural help if you chose to. That would make you as useful as Lamprey."

"Are you managing me?" he asked suspiciously.

"I wouldn't think of it," I lied. "Merely clarifying that you could be of great service in my desperate hour of need, if you felt so generously inclined."

"So you want me to fetch the lamp."

Hades! He'd never do it now. "You're too smart for me," I confessed ruefully.

"Obviously," he agreed, mellowing.

Sinbad stirred. "What?" he asked groggily.

"We got dosed and dumped," I explained. "Plot by the captain to steal the treasure."

Suddenly he was wide awake. "But I need that treasure to ransom my wife!"

"The man is a gas-bloated donkey's anal sphincter," I remarked. "He thinks he has a better use for the treasure than wasting it on a mere captive woman."

"I will tie him to the mast and flay off all his skin!"

"An admirable ambition," I agreed. "First we need to un-maroon ourselves.

Now Duban stirred. He had taken least of the doped drink, but was not hardened to alcohol or bhang. "Why do I feel as if I just vomited?" he asked.

"There was bhang in the sherbet," I told him. "We didn't know. The captain plotted to strand us and abscond with the treasure before we could spend it on a ransom."

"The Assyrians impaled people for less than that," he said, annoyed. Impalement in those old days had been a matter of sitting men on vertical pointed posts so their their own weight gradually bore them down until their ruptured guts killed them. It was one of those punishments like crucifixion that was best avoided.

"So what do we do now?" Sinbad asked, being a practical person.

I got a genius of an idea. "Duban, you still wear the silver ring?"

"Yes." He looked embarrassed. "Every so often she squeezes me, almost as if it is some other part of me she surrounds."

"She can't help it; she's a Siren. Squeezing is as natural to them as singing. But I believe we can use her, if she's willing."

Duban focused, and the ring expanded until Sylvie had joined us in the boat, lusciously naked and fully aware of it. "I'm willing," she said. "I swore an oath not to seduce Duban, but that doesn't count for the other two of you. So yes, I can divert you while you wait to die of exposure."

So she could hear and understand us while in ring form. I would keep that in mind. "I need to get a lamp from our cabin in the Fat Chance. Can you swim fast enough to catch up to the ship?"

"Certainly; a siren can outrace any ship. But you don't need lamp light; it's daytime. Even at night, we can do it by feel. If you fumble, I can guide you."

It seemed that Sirens were somewhat single minded about the interests of men, perhaps not without reason. "We're not interested in seduction at the moment," I said. "I just need that lamp."

"Oh, poo," she pouted. "I'll do it if Duban asks me to. I'm bound to him for the duration."

Duban knew about the lamp, of course. "Do it," he said.

"Immediately." She paused. "But you know I'm not conversant with the insides of ships. They're generally in bad shape by the time we get them. I could use some guidance along the way."

"We can't swim the way you can," I said.

"You won't need to. Just have Duban transform one of you into a ring, now that he knows how to do it."

We gazed at each other in wild surprise. She was right: she should have guidance, and we could do it. But who? "Me," I said before I thought. The others did not argue.

Thus it was that Duban took my hand and transformed me into a brass ring, after I stripped so as not to mess up my clothes. The process wasn't painful, merely weird, though I would have preferred to merit gold instead of brass. Sylvie put me on her middle finger, as I would have been loose on a smaller one. Then she dived into the water, her legs becoming her tail.

It was interesting the way she swam. She did not stroke with her arms, but merely held them out before her to break the water while she threshed with her powerful tail. She moved faster than any ordinary person could dream of; the spume fairly flew from her de facto prow. She wasn't even breathless from the effort; she talked to me in a normal voice.

"The Mistress likes you. She said to keep you safe as well as the boy, if I could. Our alliance would not be worth much if you died. So I'm helping you survive."

I squeezed her finger once, meaning agreement.

"You know, it would serve that nasty captain right if someone dosed *him* with bhang and marooned him," she continued. "I could do it if you approve."

Now that was a notion! I squeezed once again.

"I hated seeing the captain plot against you," she continued. "I suspected him, and tried to warn Duban, but he misunderstood my squeeze."

So that was the meaning of her communication. She had been trying to help him, not seduce him. She did not seem like a bad sort, as Sirens went.

But then she countered my thought. "You're a halfway handsome lout. Are you sure you wouldn't like me to seduce you? I could do it with my song, now that the tone-deaf spell has worn off, but Mistress said not to do it unless you actually want it."

I did not respond, though I did wonder whether her song could do it. After seeing the non-stop passion of the sailor, I was not about to bet that it couldn't.

The ship hove into view ahead. We had made amazing progress.

I anticipated a problem: Sylvie would surely be seen, and a lovely naked woman would attract immediate attention. How could we abate that?

"Good question," she said. That was when I realized that she could read my thoughts; I didn't have to be limited to squeezing. But then why hadn't she had Duban read her thoughts about the captain?

"His mind was closed to me," she said sadly. "He doesn't quite trust me."

I decided not to pursue that aspect, because I did not quite trust her either. *Find clothing,* I thought. *Avoid showing yourself before that.*

"I will try," she said.

She came to the ship, found a trailing rope, put on legs, and climbed nimbly up it. She was one strong healthy creature, a lot tougher than she looked.

"Thank you."

I stifled further thoughts.

Soon we were on the deck. We were in luck; no one was looking our way. I directed Sylvie to a storage bin where we found discarded old tattered men's clothing. She donned that, then bound back her luxurious hair. Now she looked almost like a small sailor.

We headed for our cabin. And there was a sailor pawing through our stuff. No, it was the captain himself, the one who knew (he thought) that we would not be returning. How could we get the lamp without alerting him to our presence, and to its importance?

He heard us. He looked up. He opened his mouth.

Sylvie stepped into him and closed his mouth with a kiss. I could feel his sheer amazement.

But what would happen when the kiss ended?

CHAPTER FOURTEEN

The captain, clearly surprised at having been kissed by what surely appeared to be a smallish male sailor, obviously got over his shock by returning the kiss vigorously.

As the Siren continued her embrace, I saw—or rather felt—what she was up to. With her hands entwined behind the captain's back, the cunning sea nymph began working me free from her finger.

Once the ring was free, the spell was immediately nullified and I landed hard on the wooden floor, still curled and clutching my bare toes. Hardly a position worthy of a king!

But the captain, apparently not completely lost in the luscious creature's embrace, immediately spun about at the crashing thud behind him.

"You!" he shouted, his voice rising slightly with confusion and shock. He promptly threw the sea maiden off him. She didn't go willingly and I saw the lust in her eyes. Apparently, any man would do.

I leaped to my feet—all too aware that I stood as naked as the day I was born—and faced a fully armed, battle-hardened captain. And, apparently, thief. My member, I couldn't help but notice, had all but shriveled up and disappeared. Maybe that was always its response to an inevitable fight. Disappearing from action to save itself. If so, I agreed with the instinctive action.

"How did you get back here?" he demanded, drawing his narrow scimitar, which, I suspected, he wielded expertly. "Where is Sinbad?"

My mind worked frantically. "He's here, on board, gathering the men. He's a hero to them. Much more than you, dung-face. Your ridiculous plan failed."

He cocked an ear, listening. "I hear of no activity above deck."

He was in such a position to see up through the hatch, where a short flight of stairs led to the deck. Even I could see a sailor lounging not too far away, enjoying the sun, oblivious.

He turned back to us, holding his sword steady. "I think you lie."

"We would have given you a hefty share of the profit," I said.

"Why take a share, when you can have the whole lot?"

"Spoken," I said, "like a true snake."

He pointed the tip of his sword toward Sylvie. "And where did you find this fine creature?"

I was backed up against a wall. The simple wooden box containing the magic lamp was under my cot. I could see the corner of it and so far the captain hadn't gotten his grubby hands on it.

The captain seemed intent on the Siren, for good reason. After throwing her off him, her felt hat and oversized clothing had become partially undone. Some of her female anatomy was partially spilling out. But the captain wasn't completely enchanted. He advanced toward me, for a snake such as he would first do away with me before pouncing on her.

True, he might not be fully enchanted by her, but I knew of a way he would be, and I decided I had to risk it.

"Sylvie, I want you to sing for him," I said grimly.

The captain barked with laughter. "Oh, she will sing for me soon enough—and if she values her life, she will do anything else I ask of her."

Sylvie ignored him and steadily looked at me. She knew full well the effects her voice would have on a mortal man. "Are you sure, sire?"

I nodded. "Once done, return immediately to Duban and Sinbad and lead them here."

As the captain adjusted his grip and prepared to impale me, Sylvie opened her mouth...and the most beautiful, rapturous voice I had ever heard came pouring out. Love gripped my heart. Love and lust and joy, and all thought of anything else escaped me completely. I needed the woman desperately, and never had I seen such a beautiful creature in all my existence. By Allah, I had to have her. All thoughts of Jewel fled as surely as shadows do before the light. All that filled my thoughts and heart was the beauty of this incredible creature. The longing was so great within me that I wept nearly uncontrollably.

The effect on the captain was the same, and still the Siren sang. Her voice seemed to grow louder, stronger, richer, sweeter. My entire body reacted to her, craved her, hungered for her. She was my soulmate. I was sure of it. She was my greatest heart's desire. Of that I was certain.

The captain dropped his sword. Instead he reached out with both hands open. The look on his face pure bliss. He looked how I felt. There was no jealousy. There was only her.

As she sang she backed away from us, her angelic voice vibrating the very walls of this little cabin. Now she turned and climbed the stairs, still singing.

Where was she going? Why was she leaving us?

The captain and I nearly fell over ourselves as we clambered up the stairs behind her. His hate for me, his wicked ways, my desire to thwart his nefarious plan and to help my good friend Sinbad, were all abandoned.

We knew only her song, as did now everyone else aboard, for her strong voice carried far and wide, and now the entire crew moved toward her, stupefied, filled with love and lust.

At the ship railing, she blew me a kiss—I was certain it had been for me—and she fell over backward into the water. The crew and myself all rushed to the starboard side, peering over, crying out to her. There, I saw only a flash of white as her perfect form slipped beneath the waves.

The captain immediately turned to us all. "We must find her at all costs, men!"

A great cheer arose, and my voice was perhaps the loudest of all. And we immediately set sail in the direction she had disappeared, heedless of where we were going or of our ultimate fate.

It was sometime later, with the sun setting and the ship making lackluster progress on a weak wind, that another, smaller vessel arrived. It appeared to be moving quickly, as if by magic, and I immediately recognized all aboard.

It was, of course, Duban and Sinbad. The young wizard appeared to be using an energy spell of some sort to move the small boat quickly over the waves. Once it pulled up along side, Duban appeared exhausted. Performing magic, I suspected, took great concentration.

Their arrival was met with little reaction from those on ship, myself included. We sought only the Siren, and she alone, for she filled our hearts with a longing that was stronger than anything I had ever felt in all my life.

Sinbad boarded expertly, drawing himself up a length of rope. He drew his sword, looking about confusedly. Then he saw me, standing near the single mast, holding it longingly, gazing out to sea with no doubt a very wistful look. The others on deck, I knew, had similar expression, and I only peripherally saw Sinbad look at the young man knowingly.

The sailor said to the boy, "They have been enchanted by the Siren's song. They are lost to us."

"No!" cried Duban. The boy appeared before me, tugging at the hem of my tunic. "Father! Aladdin! King Aladdin! Look at me!"

But I couldn't risk taking my eyes off the sea. What if the beautiful creature appeared and I missed her? Oh, the horror!

Never will I take my eyes off the sea again until I'm in the arms of my great love.

The boy took my hand, and I felt a great rippling of energy creep over me, and just for the smallest moment, I felt love again, but this time for Jewel. I looked down at Duban, and he smiled, relieved. But then the moment wore off, and I once again snapped my head forward, horrified that I had looked away from the sea.

By Allah, what if she had made an appearance and I missed her!

"It's too strong," said Duban. "I cannot reverse the effects."

I heard him speaking but, really, I wasn't paying attention.

Sinbad stood before me, hands on hips. He had returned his scimitar, seeing that there was no threat here. "The Lamp," he said. "Fetch me the lamp."

Duban nodded and headed off below deck. Still, I scanned the horizon. So far there was nothing. But she was near. I was sure of it. I could feel her.

The boy came back carrying the box with my lamp, but I gave it only a cursory glance. Lamps had no meaning for me. Nothing had meaning except my deep love for my creature of the deep.

Sinbad opened the box and removed the beautiful lamp. No one else on board gave us any notice; indeed, like myself, all eyes were directed forward, out to sea, searching.

"The djinn is surely powerful enough to reverse the effects of the spell," said Duban. "Except it is bound only to him."

"What do you mean, boy?" demanded Sinbad.

"It means only Aladdin can summon it and make a request of it."

Sinbad bit his lip and thought hard. I cared little for what he thought or what he did, only that they not stand in my field of vision.

Where was she? Was she safe? By Allah, I loved her….

Sinbad said, "Ask her if she can reverse the spell."

Duban shook his head. "She's keeping her distance for now, remember? She can't risk coming too close."

"Camel dung," muttered Sinbad.

And just then a great cry arose from the boat. "There!" someone shouted. "She's there!"

I rushed to the railing and saw what appeared to be a common dolphin playfully swimming alongside the ship.

"Fool!" shouted the captain.

Duban suddenly spoke up, "When I tried to reverse the spell, my father came back to us for just a few seconds."

Sinbad apparently caught on to whatever nonsense the boy was talking about. If thy weren't talking about my lovely sea maiden, then I cared little for their conversation. "Perhaps he can return to us long enough to summon the djinn and make his request."

Duban nodded. "I will increase the potency, although I am already exhausted from the energy spell to get us here."

"It is worth a try," said Sinbad.

Next I felt a familiar tingle rise up my arm, and as it did so, an image of Jewel appeared in my thoughts, and I suddenly felt a wave of guilt for loving another.

"He's back!" said Duban. "Father, take the lamp. Quickly. Summon Lamprey and reverse the Siren's spell."

Although confused and disoriented, as if being awakened from the sweetest of dreams—a dream I longed to return to—I absently rubbed the map as instructed and immediately the handsome djinn appeared before me, riding a cloud of smoke and hovering high above us.

"Your wish is my command," he said.

"Shove it, smoke face," said Duban. "Now wish it, father."

"Wish what?"

"To reverse the Siren's spell."

"Why would I want to do that?"

"Because you love mother."

"I do?"

"Yes, father. You do." And the boy grabbed my arm and sent another charge of energy up it, and my head cleared a little more. I immediately made the wish and Lamprey, now looking robust and healthy after last year's months of being tortured by another of his kind, bowed and snapped his fingers.

The spell was lifted. The fog was removed and I saw clearly where I was, although a small longing in my heart remained for the beautiful sea creature.

"You're back, father," said Duban, swinging my hand gleefully.

I was, although I felt a pang of loss for the sea creature.

"He's back," said Lamprey. "But he will always feel the effects of the Siren's call. Deep in his heart he will love her and want her, although he will not feel compelled to search for her. It will merely be a longing that can never be answered, by anyone."

"I can live with that," I said. "I think." I surveyed the deck and saw the other sailors looking yearningly out to sea. How many had turned on us? I didn't know.

Lamprey saw my look. "The Siren's magic is too powerful for me to save everyone, master. I have reached my limit for now. Remember, I am still recovering from my time spent with Prince Zeyn. I am still not at full capacity."

"Thank you, Lamprey," I said. "Begone."

The djinn bowed and disappeared; I returned the lamp to its wooden box.

"What should we do with the others?" asked Sinbad.

The others were as good as dead. After all, they would forever search for their Siren, now that they had heard her beautiful call. I spied the two rowboats tied to the hull.

"Duban," I said, "is it possible for you to determine who was in on the captain's plot?"

"I think so, father."

"Do so now."

The boy closed his eyes and turned in a small circle. "All but three, master."

"Fetch the innocent ones."

He did, and soon they stood next to me, each looking help-lessly out to sea.

Sinbad and I went to work gathering the others into the two boats and setting them on a course for Siren Rock. At least, they would die happy, which was more than they deserved. The remaining three, although worthless now, could be saved later with Lamprey's help.

Now, with the ship riding low and heavy with treasure, I looked at Sinbad. "Welcome to your new ship, captain."

CHAPTER FIFTEEN

"We need to get moving," Sinbad said. "But I don't actually know how to handle a ship. That's the captain's job, and the crew's."

"I don't either," I said. "But maybe I can get some good advice." I rubbed my brass ring.

Faddy appeared. "You know I don't have to answer your summons, mortal," he said huffily. "But if you really need advice…"

"We are incapable of sailing this ship ourselves, or of properly directing what remains of the crew," I said. "I suppose that would be too much of a challenge for you, too."

"You are managing me!" he snapped.

I put on my biggest, obviously fakest, mask of innocence. "How could I possibly do that, when you're so much smarter than I am?"

"All right!" he glowered. "I'll tell you how. Simply have your Siren beckon the remaining sailors toward Cloudland. Then they will do their utmost. It might even be sufficient."

"But her song will enchant us too," I protested.

"If you are too stupid to use the tone deaf magic."

I whacked the side of my head to knock the dottle out. "By Allah, Faddy, you really have figured it out!"

"Naturally, mortal," he agreed, trying to suppress his inordinate surge of pride. What he wanted most was respect, and in this instance we all knew he had earned it.

"Sylvie!" I called across the water.

In a moment she was there, beautifully bare in the water. "Have you suppressed my spell, Aladdin? I didn't dare return too soon, lest you dive into the water to pursue me."

"Suppressed it, mostly, yes," I agreed. "And I want to thank you for handling those sailors, Sylvie, and for helping us recover the ship."

"You're welcome," she said. "I am trying to be of service in what ways I can. Of course if you wish to take that more literally—"

It was wickedly tempting, thanks to the lingering suppressed longing of her song. But I couldn't afford it, as it would mess up our quest and might compromise my relationship with Jewel. Because I might actually make it with the Siren, which was not Jewel's intention when she referred me to a concubine. Besides, Duban was watching. "Um, no, thanks; I'd never accomplish my mission. Look, we are going to invoke the tone deaf spell again. Then please sing to the three remaining sailors. We want them to do their best to steer this ship toward Cloudland. Will you do that?"

"Gladly. Then I will need to rest; exerting my magic too long tires me."

"You will be welcome to ring my finger and rest."

She smiled, appreciating the double entendre. "That will be a pleasure for us both." More entendre. Sirens really did like to flirt.

"Give us a few minutes, then sing."

Duban was already taking up his lyre, frowning. He didn't like to see me teasing the Siren, who was definitely not any ordinary concubine, though he understood that I was managing her just as I was Faddy. A significant part of his growing up would be learning to handle the necessary compromises of life.

Soon the three of us were tone deaf. I waved to Sylvie though I could no longer see her. The song started, faintly, sounding to me like a mere moaning. What a change!

Immediately the three sailors perked up. "What's that?" one asked.

"That is the Siren," I informed them. "Singing again. I think she likes you."

We didn't have to do anything more. The three sailors worked diligently to get the sails oriented so that the ship moved toward the sound. Even when it faded, they continued, thinking that they were not keeping pace. They were not as good as a full crew would have been, but they managed.

Now that we were nearing our destination, I thought of something I should have checked before. "Sinbad, exactly how do you know your wife is here?"

"I received a message a seer assured me was authentic. This is it." He brought out a parchment.

I took it and read its brief message. SINBAD STOP YOUR WIFE SURVIVES STOP WE HAVE HER CAPTIVE STOP BRING A SUFFICIENT FORTUNE TO CLOUDLAND STOP HEREIN FAIL NOT OR SHE WILL SUFFER GRIEVOUSLY END

Bemused, I handed it to Duban. "What do you make of this?"

Duban, surprisingly, was impressed. "This thing reeks of potent magic. It is either authentic or a remarkable emulation."

"Should we trust it?"

"No. It is devious beyond my fathoming. But neither should we dismiss it. Something powerful and I fear evil is operating here."

I sighed. I was getting a bit tired of harbingers of doom. "I don't much like powerful mysteries." I returned the notice to Sinbad.

Then we saw a cloud on the horizon. Was a storm forming?

"That's Cloudland," Sylvie said behind me.

I jumped, and she laughed. "We're there!" I said, gratified.

"Soon I'll ransom my wife," Sinbad said.

"Ring me," Sylvie said to Duban.

The boy was grumpy. "Why?"

She smiled at him. "You know it is not meet for such as you to see a naked women. You might get unboyish ideas."

"Maybe you should turn her over to me for the duration," I said. "So you can avoid those ideas."

He couldn't argue, though it was clear that he secretly wished he could do exactly that. Sylvie took my hand, Duban invoked the magic, and she curled around, diminished, and wound up around my little finger. She squeezed it suggestively, already flirting.

And I could read her mind. But it was not focused on seduction at the moment. *I don't like this, Aladdin. Mistress was right: there is great danger here for you. I can feel it.*

"Nothing my scimitar can't handle, I trust," I murmured, as much to bolster my own confidence as hers.

Yes, your scimitar can't handle it. I don't know what it is, but it's awful. Aladdin, you really should turn about and go home. There is nothing for you here but doom.

But I couldn't do that. We had to save Sinbad's wife. Then we could go home.

Sylvie sighed and went to sleep, recuperating. She had done a lot of singing. I saw that this time she had curled herself backwards so that her perfect face and breasts showed clearly in miniature. She as flirting even in her sleep. Nevertheless my eyes lingered guiltily on that lovely little torso.

As we sailed on, the cloud seemed to lift and expand. It became a fog atop a mountain on a large island whose base was a green jungle. There was a town there, with a harbor. Our destination.

"It seems we didn't catch the Siren, this time," Sinbad said to the sailors. "But she is surely in the area. When we dock you may rest or take shore liberty, as you choose."

They elected to rest. Now that the siren was silent, they were aware of their extreme fatigue.

We tied up at a pier. The portly harbormaster was there to greet us. "Who are you, and what be your cargo?" he inquired.

"I am Sinbad, here to ransom my beloved wife. These are my companions Niddala and Nabud, who helped me gather the treasure."

"Welcome, Sinbad and company. We have been expecting you. This way, please."

This was entirely too easy. But what could we do? We followed the man off the pier and to a stately administration building. In its central chamber was what appeared to be an ornate metal coffin with a glass lid.

"This is an image of your wife," the harbormaster said. "She is not here, but in the cloud above. This is merely to allow you to verify that she lives, and will be delivered to you when the ransom is paid."

We went to the coffin and looked in. And I went rigid.

The sleeping woman inside was lovely beyond belief. And she was my own beloved wife, lost many years ago along with our son.

"Yes!" Sinbad said. "That is she!"

She was his lost wife too? How could that be?

"Mortal, this is mischief," Faddy murmured in my ear. He of course recognized my wife, having seen her many times in the past.

Mischief? This was disaster!

CHAPTER SIXTEEN

The woman in the glass casket was both my ex-wife and Sinbad's current wife? How could this be? Indeed, I suspected sorcery. Powerful sorcery. I thought about, and wondered of what mischief Faddy had been speaking of.

"Faddy," I said to the lesser djinn, sub-vocalizing my words so only he could hear my words. "Who, exactly, do you see here?"

"Why, a beautiful djinn maiden, of course."

I nodded and raised my voice. "Nabud, who do you see here?"

My stepson came over and looked into the glass coffin. His little jaw dropped in disbelief. "Myrrh? I don't understand!"

Just as I suspected. Magic of the strongest type. We were all seeing those women who had had the most meaning for us. For me, the woman in the glass casket could have just as easily been Jewel. Was the illusion only confined to the glass case, or was the woman herself shrouded in such magic? If so, who was she then? Was it truly Sinbad's wife? A mirage? Or something far more devious?

Sinbad had not heard any of this, so lost was he at the sight of his wife. He was touching the glass absently and whispering words only he could hear.

I motioned for the young wizard to follow me to the far side of the room, noting that the harbor master was watching us suspiciously. "It is dark magic, I said. "It's not really an image of Myrrh, or an image of my own dying wife."

"I do not understand," he said.

83

I explained to him my theory behind the image and what I had seen and what Sinbad was obviously seeing. Duban nodded. "It makes sense. What creature could invoke such magic?"

"My guess is the same creature who tried to destroy both of us," I said.

Duban set his jaw. "Prince Zeyn. I am not afraid of him."

"Good," I said. "I'm not either." Although I wasn't exactly sure of that. Heavens, on some level, even my stepson made me a little nervous. No doubt this was a common reaction to any non-magician to folk as powerful as Duban and Prince Zeyn.

"So what do we do, Father?" asked Duban.

I am always surprised when he seeks my counsel, for he is such a wise boy. But then I remind myself just that: he is just a boy, in the end, his experience and wisdom only minimal.

"Let's keep this to ourselves," I said. "It does him no harm thinking that this is his wife. And for all we know, it really is. Or she is still nearby."

"I suspect a trap," said Duban.

"So do I."

"But if we play along," said Duban. "Won't we be stepping right into it?"

"Only if we were unsuspecting," I said. "We will be ever vigilant."

I had just spoken the words when the harbor master stepped forward. "Now that you have seen her, my friends, perhaps it is time to negotiate a payment."

"I want to see her in person," said Sinbad, rising regretfully from the image. "I want to see her live."

"This is not possible," said the harbormaster.

Sinbad spun on the man, fists clenched. "And why is that?"

The harbormaster merely blinked. "Because you are all under arrest."

He clicked his fingers and men poured through the two doorways into the room, swords drawn. Instinctively, Sinbad and I drew our own weapons as the guards surrounded us.

Or, rather, tried to surround us.

Duban raised his little arms and closed his eyes and said, "Duck, Father."

I did, pulling Sinbad down with me, as a mighty shockwave rocked the air above us, bursting from Duban's hands. The men were all thrown from their feet, hurled across the room and into the far walls. And, in some cases, *through* the walls.

I loved my stepson!

I grabbed his hand and pulled him along, as Sinbad and I moved quickly through the downed men, who were not killed, merely stunned. As we raced through the wooden structure, I heard the harbormaster shouting orders for our pursuit.

Outside, I saw something that shouldn't have surprised me. Our ship was being unloaded and our three Siren-song shiphands had been slaughtered, their corpses tossed into the harbor. At least they would never again be haunted by the sweet, sweet Siren song, whose memory still haunted my thoughts.

"Where to, Aladdin?" asked Sinbad, jolting me from my reverie.

But our answer was obvious. "To Cloudland," I said.

"But how?"

I thought of the rug I had procured from the Siren's cavern, the magic carpet. "Follow me!"

And they did, and soon we had descended down upon the harbor, where most of our vast treasure, including the amber-gris, had been unloaded. The treasure was lost, no doubt. And I was beginning to suspect the payment was to the harbormaster all along, while Prince Zeyn had no use for human treasure. His true prize was control. Control of the human race, perhaps.

It was just three of us, but we were a mighty three. Sinbad and I hacked and fought our way to the ship, moving through armed men who were nowhere near as skilled with the sword. Duban played his part as well, causing havoc and confusion with his magic, and soon we were upon our vast treasure.

Seeing it all here, especially the gifts I had selected for Jewel, made my heart heavy, but there was no time for such reflections. More men were pouring down into the harbor, and I saw the concerned looks on Sinbad's and Duban's faces. After all, they did not know what magic I had up my sleeve, if any at all.

There! Amid the golden cups and priceless jewels, was the rolled up carpet, which I quickly fetched and unrolled.

"A carpet?" blinked Sinbad. "You had us risk life and limb for a carpet?"

"Not just any carpet," I said. Having already mastered such magical flight, I sat in the center of it and soon it was hovering a few feet off the ground. "Climb aboard," I said. "And I suggest you two hurry."

They did, each finding their own corner, and I gave the silent command, and soon we were soaring just above the heads and outstretched swords of the pursuing guards.

I soon angled the carpet up.

Up to Cloudland.

CHAPTER SEVENTEEN

And what a flight it was!

Sinbad had described it, but the reality was far more impressive. The base of the island was a normal tropical jungle, but close inland the mountains rose steeply toward the great capping cloud. Too steep for trees; there was only clinging brush and bare rock. But then it angled less sharply, and trees resumed. These were larger, and the higher the slope rose, the bigger the trees became, until they were giants such as I had never before seen. It almost seemed that the island must sink into the sea from the sheer weight of these monsters.

We had escaped the men, flying beyond arrow range. They had not anticipated a magic carpet. But more mischief was coming. "Look!" Duban cried.

I looked where he pointed. A huge shape was flying toward us. It was a roc bird! We could not get beyond its range.

"Maybe it's illusion," Sinbad said. "Like the one at Zombie Isle."

"That one was out of its natural territory," I said tightly. "This one isn't."

Faddy appeared. "Right, Aladdin. This one's real. They use them to ferry men and goods to Cloudland."

"Do you have a suggestion how we can deal with it?"

"If all three of you jump off the carpet, the roc may have time to catch only one or two. You're bird food."

"Begone, spook!" I snapped. He faded out with a chuckle.

Meanwhile the big bird was zooming close. "I'll jump first," Sinbad volunteered with a smile that was more like a grimace. "Maybe you can loop down to catch me before I splat on the slope."

That wasn't much help either. I thought fast. "How are you at illusion, Duban?"

"I haven't tried it."

"Try it. See if you can make us look like something uninteresting, like a flying log."

Duban didn't argue. He focused, gestured, and a giant book appeared between us and the roc.

"He meant a tree log, not a ship's log book," Sinbad said with a slightly better smile.

"I thought that was what I was conjuring," Duban said, disgruntled. "I told you, I haven't tried this before."

But it seemed the book would do. It drifted away from us, then began to fall. The roc swerved to intercept it, forgetting us for the moment. It would surely catch on soon enough, but this did give us a reprieve from immediate attack.

Now our ascent had to become vertical, because it was the tops of the trees we wanted. Their huge trunks rose into the cloud above and disappeared. It was almost as if they grew in white water, upside down, their circular cross sections plunging into the base of the level cloud.

We ascended toward that foggy layer. We hovered close beneath it.

"We'll be blind when we enter that," Duban said grimly.

"Maybe there's an avenue between cloud-banks," I said without much hope.

"The bird's back," Sinbad said. "It looks annoyed."

"Illusion books don't taste very good," Duban said, almost smiling.

"Enough with the gallows humor," I said. "We've got a problem."

Indeed, the roc was zooming toward us from below, rising like a Chinese rocket, its eyes blazing, its beak open. It was big enough to take us all in one gulp.

"If we can't see in there, neither can it," Sinbad said, looking up at the cloud-line.

I angled the carpet precipitously and shot upward into the cloud. It looked like an impending crash, but it was only mist. We were hidden. But I didn't take a chance; I veered to the side within the fog.

Sure enough, a huge shape blasted past us, the draft almost tipping us over. The roc had gone for the place we disappeared.

We all had the wit to keep silent. I steadied the carpet, and we hovered, hardly breathing.

Nothing happened. The roc had evidently lost us and flown on.

But now we were lost ourselves, having no idea where we were or where to go.

Something loomed nearby. Was it the roc? No, it was the wall-like trunk of a tree. We could vaguely see it from up close.

Well, that was a guide. "Going up," I murmured, keeping my voice low so the big bird would not orient on it.

We rose, carefully. We came to a huge branch, and guided around it. Then another, and a third. Now the fog thinned somewhat, and we could see neighboring trunks. Their lateral branches formed an increasingly thick lattice as they interwove, making a firm framework.

And here within the cloud was a city! Houses with their foundations anchored to the lattice, rising parallel to the diminishing trunks. Little light diffused here, and no direct sunlight. The walls seemed to be of translucent glass, showing vague outlines of the occupants. I could not tell whether they were human or avian or a combination. But the city itself was phenomenal, the houses connected by precarious bridges and walkways through the roiling mist. There were occasional flashes of lightning reflecting from the walls, brightening the city in the manner of a faceted diamond, followed by muted booms of thunder, and light rain fell. Now I saw that some of the buildings had adjacent gardens, with foliage hardy enough to prosper even in perpetual twilight; those plants still needed water.

"Interesting," I said. "But we're not tourists. They'll be after us soon. Where's the woman?" I carefully did not identify her, as we did not know which woman she was.

"In a cave in the highest peak of the mountain," Duban said. He evidently had a good memory for detail. "Guarded by a serpent large enough to swallow two camels whole."

"Which explains why the roc doesn't frequent this area," I said. "That serpent would not be easy prey." I was trying for a bit of humor myself, but it wasn't working well.

"And there it is!" Sinbad said, pointing.

There beyond the forest of trees and buildings was the top of the mountain, and there was a ledge around it where a serpent could slither, and the dark mouth of a cave.

Too pat, Sylvie thought. I had forgotten that I now wore her on my finger.

Thus prompted, my suspicion circuit came on. "We know this whole business is a trap," I said. "We've seen the perfidy of the natives below. Now we are seeing no one, not even the serpent. Our access to the cave is clear. What can it be except the teeth of the trap? We go there at our peril."

Sinbad looked at me, nodding. "What do you recommend?"

"That we look for the maiden elsewhere. Maybe they have her on display as a trophy. Maybe she's the plaything of the great wizard this lofty city serves. We can surprise them. They won't expect us to strike away from the cave. Maybe we can find her and carry her away before they realize."

"Maybe," Sinbad agreed uncertainly.

I steered the carpet away from the cave. At that point huge fangs appeared and the cave collapsed. It was the monstrous mouth of the serpent! We had almost flown right into it.

"I think I had better work on my repulsion magic," Duban said. "So that a mouth will not be able to crush us like mice."

"You do that," Sinbad said shakily.

90

I guided the carpet rapidly around the city, weaving between trunks and buildings. And there suddenly was a palace edifice, larger than the other buildings, its walls not translucent but transparent. Within it was a beautiful nude young woman. My lost wife.

"My wife!" Sinbad breathed.

"Myrrh," Duban said.

Just so. This was the origin of the woman we had seen below, whoever she really was. They had not hidden her in the fake cave. We had to fetch her and get her out of Cloudland. Only then could we properly question her and ascertain her true nature. After that maybe we would know what to do next.

The woman was standing before the wall, peering out. She looked unutterably sad, as if struggling not to be resigned to her fate. Obviously she could not go far, even if she escaped the palace, because of her nudity. Not that she had anything to be ashamed of there; she was as lovely a creature as had ever graced the mortal world.

*Well...*Sylvie thought.

"Next to you," I murmured, rubbing a finger over the ring.

She inhaled. Or at least her breasts seemed to become larger. I quickly removed my finger. She seemed to be satisfied, regardless.

Then I saw a robed man walking along a transparent hall. He was coming toward the room where the woman was confined. The evil wizard!

I did not pause to think. "Cover your faces!" I yelled. "Hang on!" I propelled the carpet at the glass wall, bracing for the impact.

The glass shattered, shards flying everywhere, but we were not cut. I landed the carpet before the woman. "Come with us!" I told her.

"Aladdin!" she cried gladly.

"Yes, Rosebud!" I agreed as gladly. For her name was Buddir al-Buddoor, and I had called her by her pet name

But even as I spoke, so did Sinbad and Duban.

"Yes, Vania," Sinbad was saying.

"Yes, Myrrh," Duban said.

Not only did she look like each of our first loves, she sounded like them, and knew our names. This would take some sorting out.

"Aladdin, beloved," Rosebud said urgently. "Do not touch me! It's a trap! I am horribly enchanted. Fly away from here before the Wizard binds you with webs of sinister magic."

But we were already crowding around her as the glass door opened and the Wizard entered. "Halt!" he shouted, raising his hands to cast a spell.

We put our arms around the woman protectively.

And suddenly we were elsewhere. We stood embracing her in a land with odd vegetation. I recognized it instantly. "Djinnland!"

"They enchanted me as a portal between the realms, just as the serpent was," Rosebud said sadly. "Now you are truly trapped. I would have spared you this if I could. I am so very, very sorry, my love."

She was hardly the only one.

CHAPTER EIGHTEEN

"What is this place?" asked Sinbad, stunned. Duban's mouth also dropped open in amazement. We seemed to be in a clearing, surrounded by trees with purple trunks. Large, lumbering bees buzzed by us, their stingers long enough to poke one's eye out.

I told them both of Djinnland, where humans were so dense that we tended to sink into the ground, where marvelous creatures such as flying dragons lived, and where magic was commonplace.

"But we are not sinking now," said Duban.

"That's because we are standing on bedrock. But don't be fooled. The moment you step onto softer ground, you will sink as surely as a stone would in the ocean."

"But how do we move if we're trapped in the earth?" asked Sinbad with a note of panic in voice. I did not blame him. For a seafaring man, this would surely be his worst nightmare.

"Not trapped," I said, and explained that since we were far heavier than the surrounding landscape we would be able to move easily through the earth itself, but only along the solid bedrock below.

"So we travel with the worms and other foul creatures?" asked Duban.

"It serves a purpose for concealment," I said. "But there is another way." I next told them of the technique Jewel and I had devised, wherein we held thoughts of lightness—images of mist or clouds or even of the air itself—to buoy our own bodies.

"And this technique worked?" asked Sinbad skeptically.

"More often than not."

"Gentleman," said my deceased wife, Rosebud. "Need I remind you that the three of you have fallen victim to a devious trap. I strongly suggest we get moving."

"But where to, my love," said Sinbad, immediately taking my deceased wife's hand. Of course, he was seeing his once missing wife, as Duban was seeing his own first love.

An odd jealousy rose up within me, one that bypassed my logical mind and went straight for the heart. How dare Sinbad take my wife's hand!

"Snap out of it, human," whispered Faddy in my ear. "Remember, she is part of a devious plot to destroy you and take over your kingdom."

"But I miss her so much."

"Of course you do, simpleton. Tread carefully, lest you be stung."

I looked away from the image of Sinbad holding my deceased wife's hand. "I think I liked you better when you called me master," I said, grumbling.

Faddy laughed, and not pleasantly. "You have been warned."

"Warning heeded," I said, as a question occurred to me. "Can you tell me why Prince Zeyn didn't transport us into his dungeon? Why here?"

"How do you know Prince Zeyn is behind this mischief?"

"Is it someone else?"

"Of course not, buffoon! Who else but Prince Zeyn could lure you here?"

"You're wasting my time," I growled under my breath.

"And time is something you most certainly do not have. To answer your question: Although the dark prince has the means to transport you here, he has no control where you will ultimately appear. Those bees you saw earlier? Those are his eyes and ears."

"So he knows where we are?"

"Oh, yes, he and his men will be here shortly."

"Don't sound so pleased," I grumbled.

"The only pleasure I receive is watching your simple mind work. Case in point, Prince Zeyn isn't the only djinn around who could transport you here."

"Lamprey!" I said, realizing my fatal error. "Oh, camel dung!"

"Ah, so you're only now realizing that you left your precious djinn back on the ship with the other treasure. Treasure that even now is being sorted through by Prince Zeyn's men."

"I'm a horrible master!"

"Indeed, Aladdin. It appears your Lamprey will once again find himself imprisoned. That is, if he's not saved in time. Help, after all, is on its way."

"What do you mean? Will you help fetch Lamprey?"

"You are even more simple than I thought."

Yes, I could see now my error: was Faddy too jealous of the powerful djinn to help him? "Out with it, Smoke Face."

"Your wife is on the way."

"Jewel?"

"She is your wife, is she not?"

"I do not understand."

"Of course not, dog, so let me explain it to you clearly. The queen has been using me as a spy, and with great pleasure I have been reporting your roguery and dalliances."

"No wonder why you were so willing to come around, despite having been freed. You were spying! Why, you two-faced—"

"Now, now, my lord. She is just a concerned wife. And lucky for you. She is, even now, arranging to rescue the lamp and, in turn, you."

"Alone?"

"Of course not. She will be traveling with an intrepid thief who hails from Baghdad."

"The Thief of Baghdad!"

"Yes, as he's commonly called. Quite a handsome and dashing fellow from what I understand. He was recently arrested and presented to court. From what I gather, Jewel was quite smitten with him, as were all the women. Anyway, it appears that he's agreed to help fetch your magic lamp in return for his freedom."

I felt the heat rise to my face. How much of what Faddy said was true, I didn't know, as the ifrit seemed inclined toward mischief of late. Still, I had to believe that Jewel was on her way to Cloudland in search of the magic lamp. And she was traveling with the notorious Thief of Baghdad.

"Begone," I said irritably to Faddy, whose presence faded away with a chuckle. Perhaps I should never have freed him.

"You were speaking with your ifrit," said Rosebud, moving over to me. Sinbad trailed close behind.

"Er, he's not my ifrit. Not anymore."

"Then why does he still report to you?"

"Never mind that," I snapped, facing her, my anger rising. Whoever she was, she meant us harm. But my ire abated immediately upon looking into my wife's beautiful, almond-shaped eyes. Eyes I had not seen in many, many years. I looked away. "We have to get moving."

"Indeed," said Sinbad, taking his wife's hand protectively. "We need to escape this land. But how?"

How indeed? How should I tell Sinbad that he had most certainly *not* taken the hand of his wife, that she was no doubt Prince Zeyn's prisoner here in Djinnland, if she was alive at all.

I didn't know, but as I looked into the far distance, I saw a great cloud forming in the sky, a cloud that looked suspiciously like the face of Prince Zeyn.

And it—or he—was approaching quickly.

We had to run. But to where?

CHAPTER NINETEEN

"**B**etter think of something soon," Sinbad said. Duban remained distracted by the mystery woman. Naturally it was up to me to rescue us all. Somehow it generally seemed to be that way.

And I had no idea. My mind was a blank wet blanket. That, too, was typical.

Aladdin.

It was Sylvie Siren, wrapped around my finger. "You can help?" I asked without real hope.

Restore me. I will sing my song and lead your nemesis away while you escape.

"And what will happen to you when the foul lord catches you?" I asked. "He will not be kind to you."

That's not the point. I want to help you, and this is the only way I know.

"Forget it," I said. "I don't want to send you into ugly slavery and doom." If I had had time to examine my motives, I might have discovered that it was the lingering fascination of her song that made me loath to hurt her. Fortunately I lacked that time.

Meanwhile the cloud loomed closer. It was definitely Zeyn.

My eye fell on the mystery maiden. She had conjured us here, but obviously not by her choice. She had tried to warn us away, and expressed her regret. So she was not our enemy. But who was she?

Let me touch her, Sylvie thought. *I will fathom her identity.*

I put out my hand and grasped the maiden's arm, the ring touching her flesh. She stiffened, aware of the touch.

Got it, Sylvie thought. *She is Nydea Nymph, of the tribe of Nubile Nymphs. They are cousins of ours, only their point in existence is to make men happy without harming them, in contrast to our way. They are nicer than we are. Their inherent magic is to resemble any man's most beloved image, to better serve his need. She was lured to Prince Zeyn's castle on the promise of excellent prospects for marriage, as only by marriage to a mortal can a Nubile Nymph achieve mortality herself, her fondest wish. But it was a ruse; she was captured and then enchanted to spring the trap. She is horribly grieved. It is not her nature to harm any mortal man.*

Nydea turned to me. "You have a captive siren!" she said.

"Not captive," I said. "She associates with us by choice. She says you're a victim too."

Now the cloud was almost upon us. "Can you fight him off?" Sinbad asked Duban.

"In the mortal realm, yes," the boy answered. "But here in his realm he is stronger than I am. It is me he really wants to capture and kill."

"I am a victim too," Nydea agreed sadly, on our separate dialog.

But her people live here in Djinnland," Sylvie thought. *They have a refuge safe from the evil prince. That's why he doesn't like them, and abuses them when he can.*

A refuge! Suddenly my lagging brain functioned. "Take us to your leader!" I told Nydea.

"But there is no time," she protested. "The monster is about to grab us all."

"Not if we dive underground."

"I can't do that! I'm not mortal."

"You're a cousin species to the Sirens," I said persuasively. "Can you change form?"

"No. Only my aspect, as men gaze at me. That's appearance rather than reality."

But I had an answer. "Duban!" I snapped. "Change this woman into a ring."

He stared at me. "But—"

"Now!"

Bemused, he obeyed. In moments Nydea was another ring, on my finger adjacent to Sylvie, still looking like my beloved. I had to keep my eye off her, lest I be overcome by nostalgia. "Which way?" I asked.

That way, she thought, mentally indicating a direction. She, too, was bemused by the transformation.

"Follow me!" I cried, changing in that direction as the vile cloud descended on us.

We ran off the surface bedrock and into the softer ground. I could see that both Sinbad and Duban were amazed, but I didn't have time to explain it further. Soon we were in over our heads, forging along the buried bedrock.

Above the ground the cloud raged, powerless to catch us. We had escaped, for the moment.

I hoped the way to Nubile Refuge would remain underground throughout. Because I knew the angry cloud was following us. Our density protected us from Zeyn at the moment, but the instant we surfaced he would be on us, and woe betide us then!

While I ran I pondered. If we were so firmly trapped in Djinnland, why was Prince Zeyn so eager to get hold of us? Why wasn't he going after the Lamp, which was surely more of a threat to him? Then I remembered what Duban had said: *he* was the one Zeyn was really after. In the mortal realm Duban was, when aroused, stronger than Zeyn. But in Djinnland he wasn't. But maybe he could become so, if given time. So he needed to be dispatched immediately. No good to secure the Lamp if the Boy was developing dangerous power here. That explained our predicament, and suggested that we might have a winning cast of the dice if we could just survive the moment.

And while we distracted Zeyn, Jewel was on her way to recover the Lamp. But there was a problem there: we had sailed at least a week's distance from our port, the same one she would have to use. It would take her a week to get there. That was far too much time.

Perhaps not, Sylvie thought. *She's with the Thief of Baghdad. We know of that scoundrel. Last year he secretly plugged his ears, faked fascination, and stole an invaluable high-speed magic carpet from us. He surely has it now, and that will enable them to reach the ship within a day.*

We know of him too, Nydea thought. *He thieves hearts, too. He is to be trusted only as a betrayer.*

And this wretch was traveling with my wife.

But first things first. We had to save our hides, or the Thief would be the least of our concerns.

"Your home. Refuge," I said to Nydea. "It really is safe from the wrath of Prince Zeyn?"

Yes. But the moment we leave it, he can stalk us and sometimes capture us. So we have very little effective power.

"And you know the sirens? How is this, if you reside in Djinnland and they reside in the mortal realm?"

We have portals to other realms we can use. Like the one between your realm and this one, that Zeyn forced me to use. So we associate with the sirens, with whom we get along well.

We do, Sylvie agreed.

Aha. "So you could connect us to our ship?"

It is not that easy. We don't make portals, we use them. Zeyn made the one he fastened me to. And while the portals may be safe for us to use, that would not be true for mortals. There are nasty beasties along the way.

I had had some experience with the type. Still, it started devious plans stirring in my brain. "Is there a portal to Hades?"

There is, but Aladdin, beloved, you must not venture near that one! There is no return!

Precisely. "And can you emulate a man?"

100

Both ring maidens were shocked. *Aladdin, your passion is not for a man!* Sylvie protested.

"Indeed not," I agreed. "But *could* you?"

If a man truly desired another man, we could reflect that, Nydea agreed reluctantly. *At least our queen Nylon could. She has better control over our nature, and more, um guts.* She was a nice girl and did not like to use the crude term.

"Zeyn's passion right now is Duban. He wants to capture and kill him. Could you emulate Duban when Zeyn pounces?"

I think so. But such a deception could not fool Zeyn long.

"And could your emulation of Duban stand astride the portal to Hades?"

Aladdin, you are frightening us, Sylvie thought.

But it is a good fright, Nydea thought.

"I want to send Zeyn to Hades. Then all the rest will become academic."

Academic, Sylvie thought. *You must have attended some academy!*

Now we came to a broad passage underground, leading to a shimmering portal. My beloved Rosebud stood guard there, with truly shapely legs. "Who are you?" she demanded as we emerged into that passage.

I removed the Nydea ring. She reformed. Now there were two Rosebuds. "Queen Nylon! He is Aladdin!" she said. "He and his friends are here as refugees from Zeyn!"

"So that's what stirred up that evil ifrit! Of course we'll succor them." It seemed the queen was nice too.

More nymphs appeared. One took Duban's hand, and I knew she looked to him just like Myrrh. Nydea took Sinbad's hand, and she was his beloved wife. And Queen Rosebud, I mean Nylon, took mine. Her hand felt exactly like that of my lost beloved.

Speechless, we passed though the portal and entered the Refuge.

CHAPTER TWENTY

We were in what appeared to be the inside of a great mountain.

Surrounding us on all sides were great, sloping cliffs that came together high above. Glowing lanterns hovered in the sky, illuminating the interior.

We followed a path from the portal, down a rocky trail, and through dense jungle. Like green snakes, curious vines dropped down from branches around us. Some vines curled playfully around our arms and wrists. Although playful now, I suspected these vines could just as easily strangle or trip or even tear apart a man.

Nylon saw my amazement as one such vine playfully caressed my cheek. "Yes, our land is alive in every sense of the word. Here we call it The Refuge, but in the mortal realms, it is sometime referred to as Eden, for you are not the first humans to visit."

Sylvie, who was still on my finger, giggled as one such vine entwined through my fingers…and around her.

We continued through the forest, which parted before our large party, and then just as quickly closed behind us. Soon the dense foliage opened up to a grassy clearing, where there were many simple wooden structures. Beautiful nymphs were everywhere, tending gardens, bathing nude in steaming pools, or coming and going from the huts. I realized, with some fascination and concern, that all of them resembled my departed wife.

No doubt they all resembled Sinbad's missing wife and Duban's first love, too.

Once in the village, Nydea led Sinbad off to a hut, and the sailor willingly followed. I was about to call after them when the village leader stopped them. "Leave them be, Aladdin."

"Where is she taking him?"

"To mate with him."

I think my jaw dropped open. "But he is a married man!" I protested.

"No," said Queen Nylon. "He's not."

"I don't understand."

"Come, then let me explain."

She led me to an official-looking building, bigger than the others and made of stone. A central fire blazed inside and everywhere there were beautiful replicas of my Rosebud.

We sat next to the fire, on cushions made of straw and hides. Immediately food appeared by other nymphs, all of them identical to my lost wife. And array of meats and vegetables were offered to us. Now this felt more like home, where I, as king, was waited on hand and foot.

"So explain," I said to the nymph queen. "But first, is there a way to turn your magic off, so that you don't all look like my beloved?"

She shook her sadly. "We have little direct control over how you view us."

"Fine," I said, tearing meat off a leg bone of what I assumed was something of the size and shape of a chicken. Duban ate hungrily next to me.

"Sinbad's wife was killed not too long ago, attempting to escape Prince Zeyn."

My heart sank for my friend. "You speak the truth?"

The Queen looked stricken by my question. Sylvie came to my rescue, squeezing my finger gently. *She cannot lie, my king. She has been created to please man, and lying would never please a man.*

I understood.

"Nydea was captured once Sinbad's wife was killed. We believe accidentally, but with Zeyn one never knows. His evil knows no limit."

I nodded, catching on. "So Nydea, being enchanted, would appear to be his wife," I said, tossing aside the greasy bone. A fiery creature, shaped vaguely like a dog, appeared from the flames, snatched the bone in mid-air, and returned to the pit, where creature and bone disappeared. I stared briefly in disbelief.

The queen nodded sadly. "A magical replacement. Nydea was no doubt treated terribly, subjected to all sorts of torture and rape, only to be used as a pawn for the evil djinn." The queen absently reached out toward the fire, and the hellhound's head appeared from the flames. She scratched between its fiery ears with no ill effects. Nymphs, of course, were immortal, and apparently fire did not harm them. She went on, "And all Nydea wanted to do was look for a mate. Do you see where I'm going with this, Aladdin?"

I cudgeled my balky brain but, alas, her words were lost on me.

"Think, father," said Duban, shaking his head pathetically at his old man. "Sinbad lost his wife and Nydea was looking for a husband..."

I slapped my own forehead. "By Allah, it's a devious plan!"

"Is it?" asked Queen Nylon. "Now Sinbad will never, ever lose his wife, who will age gracefully with him, who will absorb all of his own memories of his wife, who will naturally take on the mannerisms, memory and personality of his wife. In every way, she will become his lost wife and she will never be happier. Sinbad, too, will never be happier. For remember, nymphs are created to please their man in every way imaginable."

I nearly covered Duban's ears, but already the boy had lost interest. Instead, he was playing with the hellhound, which was making me nervous. But Duban, although not quite as powerful in Djinnland as he was in the mortal realm, seemed to have created a spell to protect his hands. A fiery tail wagged happily.

"So there is no harm, and Sinbad will never know the difference. Nydea will have her dream to mate with a mortal, and Sinbad will have the love of his life."

Sylvie squeezed my finger. *Unless you prefer to tell Sinbad that his real wife was killed by the prince and crush him for the rest of his mortal life.*

I saw the benefit of not telling, and I even saw the tragic beauty of the plan. It was obvious how much the sailor loved his wife. And seeing Rosebud now conjured feelings in me that had long since lain dormant. But I had the benefit of knowing that the queen and her court were illusions.

I nodded. "I shall keep the secret, as will Duban."

The queen looked greatly relieved. "I think it is best, too. In time, her magical charm will wear off, and others, too, will see her only as Sinbad's wife."

"There is only, then, the matter of dealing with Prince Zeyn."

"A dangerous task," said the queen, "and one that many here in Djinnland have set out to do, but to only fail. Many bodies line his castle walls, where he displays the corpses for all Djinnland to see."

Next drinks were served and I quite enjoyed the spicy punch. Duban ran off to play in the woods with another nymph, whom I was assured would act appropriately for a child his age.

Nydea next arrived without Sinbad who, she claimed, was sleeping contentedly. With her hair askew, I had no doubt the exhausted sailor was sleeping deeply, completely spent and exhausted. That Nydea looked like Rosebud should have triggered feelings of jealously, but already I was getting used to the notion of the nymphs appearing to be my first true love.

With Duban playing in the woods and Nydea swimming in a natural pool with other naked nymphs, Queen Nylon sat a little closer to me and rested her hand on my thigh. "But you are safe here, King Aladdin, for as long as you wish to stay. Do you not find me satisfying?"

"You are an illusion. Truth be known, I have no clue what you look like."

"Oh, on our own we are natural beauties, my king. Our flesh is soft and our hips are curved and our breasts are wonders to behold."

I swallowed hard and slipped from under her arm. "True, you do look like my first love. But I have another love. A second great love, and she is not you, and you will never be her."

"Oh?"

And suddenly Rosebud seemed to undulate, as if under water, and the Queen who once appeared to be Rosebud now looked exactly like Jewel. "I'm not the queen for nothing, Aladdin. Unlike my maidens, I can take on other forms as I see fit."

I swallowed hard. Jewel now stood before me. Or the illusion of Jewel. My wife was a stunningly beautiful woman. The queen now dropped her robe and Jewel was standing before me completely naked, her round breasts reflecting the central fire.

I had been away at sea for a long, long time.

My body reacted instantly to the naked nymph who looked like my present wife. Who appeared exactly like my beloved wife.

"I see I got your attention, King Aladdin."

And now the Queen Nylon reached over and cupped me gently. I had just reached for her hand to push her away, when she lowered her soft mouth onto mine. And despite myself, despite the knowledge that I was kissing an illusion, I reacted passionately, loving, excitedly to the naked woman who now wrapped herself around me in the most loving embrace I had ever experienced.

And that's when I heard a gasp from a doorway, and it took all my will power to tear my lips away from Jewel's—or Queen Nylon. Standing there, face twisted with jealousy and a sword in his hand, was Sinbad.

The sailor charged me, growling with fury.

CHAPTER TWENTY-ONE

Nylon glanced at the enraged sailor without alarm. "I will handle this," she murmured. "Keep your gaze on me, not on him; do not waver." I was so badly out of sorts that I froze in place, not wanting either to fight my friend or disabuse him of the status of his wife. It was not easy to keep looking at my simulated wife when we were being attacked, but I managed it.

As Sinbad came up to us, scimitar swinging, Nylon smiled at him. I watched peripherally, nervously. "What can I do for you, my good man?"

And I believe Sinbad's mouth dropped open as his sword lowered. "I—I thought you were someone else. My apology."

"Obviously," Nylon agreed. "We Nubile Nymphs do tend to get mistaken for others. But as you can see, I am not your love, who would never betray you with another man. You know that, don't you? You will find her back where she was."

"Yes." Sinbad backed off, then turned and strode rapidly away, obviously embarrassed. Now I was free to look directly. I saw a Nymph hurrying to intercept him; Nydea must have misjudged how long he would sleep. She surely would not do that again.

"What did you do?" I asked.

"I showed him Jewel, as I am showing you. When two men gaze at me simultaneously, I can choose whose beloved to emulate. As I said, I am not Queen for nothing."

"That's why you told me to keep looking at you," I said, belatedly catching on. "Had I looked away—"

"I would have been helpless to avoid the aspect of his beloved. Then it might have become complicated."

Complicated indeed! I would have had to fight my friend, and though I was satisfied I could best him at swords, I did not want to do that. Neither did I want to kill him or allow him to kill me. Queen Nylon had spared me that dreadful choice. I shook my head, bemused. "You are some woman!"

"Indeed. Shall we resume where we left off?"

But the interruption had restored some of my senses to me. "No. You look like Jewel, but I know you are not. I know she is alive. It would be cheating to make out with you."

"Ah, but you are royal. Surely you have concubines. They are not considered cheating."

"You are no concubine!"

She shrugged. "I will take that as a compliment. A concubine is a lesser creature, there purely for your passing pleasure. I am a queen, a person of stature, so you can not be casual with me. Still, if you should change your mind, I remain interested. It is of course my nature to be interested, and I have not encountered a man of your caliber in some time."

"Thank you," I said awkwardly. I did remain interested; that was the problem. Her beauty, her power, and her flattery were all too conducive. So I changed the subject. "I have not encountered your name before. What is its origin?"

She smiled, relaxing. Unfortunately that was just as sexy as when she was coming on to me, maybe by no accident. She was a creature in search of mortal love, however rational her manner. She probably had not given up on me.

You bet, Sylvie thought. *Never trust a woman.*

Should I trust you?

Of course not! she thought indignantly. *I believe I have a prior application for seducing you, and will do so when the occasion permits.*

I shook my head, uncertain how to respond to that.

"If you are quite through conversing with your captive Siren," Nylon said, "I will answer your question."

I'm not captive!

She's teasing you.

"Of course I am," Nylon agreed. "We cousin-species Nymphs have a certain competitive camaraderie. As you know, we are immortal, and desire above all else to become mortal, normally by marrying a mortal and acquiring part of his soul."

"And that's another question," I said. "Why would anyone sacrifice immortality?"

"Because we are blank. We lack the extraordinary passions of mortality. We do not fear pain or loss or humiliation or even death. We are as empty shells." She grimaced prettily, her face now a cross between Rosebud and Jewel. "In fact we are bored as Hades. What good is immortality without love, hate, fear, hope, or joy? Our existence is interminably dull, and there is no escape from it. Except to interact briefly with mortals, borrowing their emotions, striving to make them our own, at least for the instant that is their sojourn in life."

This was interesting. "So when you seek sex with a man, you don't have lust of your own. It is all about evoking his passion so you can share a bit of the feeling."

"Exactly." She eyed me again. "Understanding that, will you now have mercy on me and let me evoke yours? I have the longing of centuries to slake."

I shook my head. "I can't. You make me feel guilty, but I can't."

"Guilt is another emotion I would gladly share with you." She sighed. "But I must answer your question. Immortality extends into the past as far as the mind can compass. It also extends into the future. Some centuries hence there will come a new material, underived from sheep or plants or flesh; it is magically processed from the inanimate substance of the ground, and spun into fine strands that can make exquisite and strong threads and textiles. Young women will wear tight stockings made of this material, enhancing their legs phenomenally, as you can see." She lifted her legs, parted toward me so that I could see every part of them from feet to juncture. They had a remarkable smoothness and luster, and of course strongly excited my masculinity yet again. "I am wearing nylon, and I take my name from it, appreciating its quality."

I appreciated it too. "I wish I could get stockings like that for my wife. She would absolutely adore them."

"I will give you these. Just let me get them off." She set about unrolling the material from her luscious legs, making sure I got to see every portion of her marvelous nether architecture. In due course she had the sheer material off, and my manhood gave scant evidence it had ever been limp. She handed the stockings to me.

They were curiously slight, weighing next to nothing. I could squeeze them into a tiny ball. Amazing how such small things could enhance such shapely limbs! I put them in a pocket. "Thank you."

"For the nylons?"

"That, too," I said, finally wrenching my gaze from her inviting cleft.

She knew she had me ready to topple. "Then let's—"

Sinbad returned, this time with Nydea. "I am taking my wife home," he said.

So his denial was complete. He had to know she was really a Nubile Nymph, but his desire for his wife was so great that he chose belief over knowledge. As Queen Nylon had pointed out, this was surely best for him.

But Nylon, surprisingly, had a caveat. "Make Refuge your home, Sinbad. You can be safe here."

"With every Nymph imitating my love? I think not. I want to be alone with my true love."

Now Duban spoke; I had not noticed when he reappeared. "It is not safe out there. Zeyn lurks. We must wait until he tires of watching."

"He wants you, not me," Sinbad said. "I mean to find a portal and return to the ship. The treasure may be gone, but I have all the treasure I need." He put his arm around Nydea, who of course did not argue. She had become Sinbad's wife, to the extent feasible, and supported him in all things.

I exchanged a frustrated glance with Nylon. What could we do in the face of this delusion?

"Maybe if we show ourselves at one portal, distracting Zeyn, they can escape by another," Duban said uncertainly.

"That would be risky for both parties," Nylon said. "Zeyn may have traps by the portals."

"And maybe he doesn't," Sinbad said. "We're going." He set off along the path that had brought us here, and Nydea went with him.

"This is catastrophe," I muttered.

"I had no idea he was so headstrong," Duban said.

"He is in love," Duban's companion said. In my distraction I had not noticed her either.

"It's an adult folly, Myrrh," Duban said.

She merely squeezed his arm agreeably. I wondered what the real Myrrh would think of this. Did the Nymph intend to remain with him until the two of them met?

She remains with him until the issue of his relationship with the real one is settled, Sylvie thought. *The real one could die, and then the Nymph could painlessly take her place. In the interim she has the pleasure of his company.*

So it seemed. Meanwhile Sinbad was marching resolutely toward likely disaster.

We had to do something to stop this idiocy. But what? As usual, my mind was freezing up.

CHAPTER TWENTY-TWO

They moved quickly together through the living forests, whose branches and vines parted obligingly. Still, a livid Sinbad brushed them away angrily when one or two curious vines reached out to him.

Soon he was at the stone path, having ignored me the entire way. The man was headstrong and foolish, and I was beginning to see why he often came back empty-handed, having lost ship, treasures and his men. He was truly lucky to be alive.

At the portal he turned to me, holding out his sword. "Do not follow me, King Aladdin. I thank you for your companionship and courage. The goal was always to save my wife, and I have done so. I only want to be far away from these enchanted vixens."

"And where will you go, friend?" I said calmly.

He gripped his Nydea's hand possessively. Nydea, of course, looked exactly like my departed wife. My head hurt. Sinbad said, "Another land. Another ship. Just far, far away."

"So this is it, then?" I said. "This is where our adventure ends?"

"It was never an adventure for me, King Aladdin. It was a rescue."

Nydea held Sinbad's hand tightly. That she would play the role of his wife admirably, I had no doubt, but something felt off here. Perhaps it was the knowledge that Sinbad was being deceived.

Do not be too hard on yourself, my lord, came Sylvie's faint voice in my thoughts. *On some level, Sinbad is aware of the deception and chooses to permit it. As admirable as her imitation is, Nydea has not yet mastered his wife's nuances. Sinbad's confusion over this is also driving his hostility and recklessness.*

So what do you suggest I do? I thought. *And how do you know this about Sinbad? You only have access to my thoughts.*

I have not lived this long for nothing, my lord. I know the ways of man, especially men in love. For we of the Sirens prey on such vulnerabilities, whereas the Nymphs exploit them.

I must admit, their way of exploitation is preferable to yours.

Oh? Do you not remember your sailor friend? He did not appear to be complaining.

Despite myself, I nearly laughed.

And to answer your question, my lord. Leave him be. He is his own man, free to love whom he chooses.

I nodded, seeing the wisdom of her words. I reached out a hand and Sinbad clasped it.

"I wish you calm seas and safe passage, my friend," I said.

He smiled and nodded. "As well you, my king. My advice is to return to your kingdom with your boy. Leave this madness behind."

"I will keep that in mind, Sailor," I said. First, of course, I would seek Jewel and Lamprey.

Recalling our own harrowing escape from Djinnland, I asked Sinbad how he and Nydea planned to return to the mortal realm. I was, of course, careful to use his wife's name, Vania, lest I wanted another quarrel with the sailor.

Instead, Nydea answered, sounding exactly as my deceased wife would have sounded. "There is a nearby enchanted cave, known only to us Nymphs. From there, we Nymphs can pass into the mortal realm with ease, although, once there, we generally appear as invisible. It is only when we have found true love—or through dark sorcery, as you have seen—that we become truly physical beings...and ultimately mortal, our fondest wish."

"And you can return my good friend with you?" I asked.

She nodded and looked up at Sinbad. "If we have found love," she said, and he squeezed her hand with obvious adoration.

I saw the Nymph's dilemma. They appeared as invisible in the mortal realm, and it seemed highly unlikely that a mortal would find their hidden realm. Indeed, it appeared Sinbad's and Nydea's union was a match ordained by Allah himself.

"I bid thee well, my friend. Godspeed." I clapped Sinbad on the shoulder and he gave me a final, bittersweet smile, and told me to look out for my boy, that he was a good lad and would make a fine musician. I noted that he didn't say ruler or magician.

Holding hands, they stepped together through the shimmering portal and into the broad passage that appeared dug from the earth itself. They were still far underground, too far for even Prince Zeyn to reach.

As they moved further down the tunnel, I was about to turn back to Nylon, who was waiting behind me, when I felt a great rumbling.

An earthquake?

Rock and other debris shook free from the slope, rattling past me. Through the shimmering portal, I saw Sinbad and Nydea pause as well, clearly confused.

I was just about to wave them back through the portal, when a great beast burst through the tunnel wall.

By Allah, it was a massive earthworm, bigger than even the lion-serpent we had encountered some time ago. The great worm opened its black maw, swallowed Sinbad and Nydea whole, and continued through the opposite wall, the great expanse of its body following, as the ground shook harder than ever, and it was all I could do to keep my footing on the rocky slope.

The rumbling faded, and I stood there in stunned silence, when Nylon ran forward, screaming. She was about to dash through the shimmering portal but stopped herself. A good idea; she was safe on this side.

Furious, she turned to me and said, "That was no worm!"

I nodded, my stunned brain finally kicking into gear. I had seen the dark prince's handiwork when he had morphed into a giant castle and a dragon. I wondered how Sinbad and Nydea were faring in the bowels of the great worm.

"Prince Zeyn," I said.

I noticed Duban and his Nymph were at the foot of the rocky path. He was out of breath. Evidently the boy had felt the rumbling and had come running.

"It could be none other." She clenched her fists, still, looking and now acting, like Jewel. "I swear this, he will never again harm another of my daughters."

"Where would he take them?" I asked.

"His castle," said Nylon.

"A real castle or an illusion?" I asked, recalling the magical illusion that had been Zeyn's castle last year.

"As real as they get. And as horrific."

I looked at her sharply. "What does that mean?"

"His castle is not only lined with the corpses of those who have opposed him, but embedded within the very walls themselves is an army of demons."

"I do not under—"

"Demons and other foul creatures lie dormant within his walls, appearing only as stone statues until called upon by Prince Zeyn." She looked at me and took my hand. "They also act as his eyes and ears, so no one can get close to Prince Zeyn without their knowledge. No one."

I set my jaw and looked back through the shimmering portal. "And this is where he took my friend?"

"And my daughter," she said. "He must be destroyed."

I couldn't have agreed more.

CHAPTER TWENTY-THREE

M y mind was blank again, so I turned to Duban. "We have
here a man-sized challenge," I told him. "To rescue our
foolish companion. Do you have any feasible ideas?"

"Yes."

"Because this is the occasion to really wrack our brains in
the faint hope of just barely possibly coming up with something
that might diminish our hopelessness in the face of—" I paused.
"What did you say?"

"He said yes, Aladdin," the Nymph with Duban answered.
"He's very smart. I mean to marry him some day."

Of course she wasn't fooling Duban, any more than Nylon
was fooling me. But their semblances were a pleasant interim
fiction, and they did mean well, so I played along. "And what do
you believe his idea is, Myrrh? Maybe you can read his mind." I
hoped I wasn't being unkind; the real Myrrh could have done
that, but not this one.

"I have asked Myrrh to stay out of my mind for the duration,"
Duban said. "I prefer to maintain my privacy, and she honors that."

The Nymph squeezed his arm affectionately, appreciating
the way he covered for her. It occurred to me that at such time
as Duban achieved his majority, he might elect to have a concubine, and the Nymph would be ideal. She would emulate his love
without the awkwardness of reading his mind.

But at the moment we had a formidable task to accomplish.
"And that idea is?"

"To give ourselves up to Prince Zeyn."

"Duban, have you lost your mind?" the emulation of Jewel, his mother, demanded, sounding just like her.

Duban looked startled, and I knew Nylon was showing him Jewel, enabled by my gaze on her. "I hope not," he said. "I am thinking that we should offer to exchange ourselves for Sinbad and Nydea/Vania. Only when Zeyn releases them do we enter his castle."

"Oh, he would certainly make that exchange," Nylon agreed. "He wants Aladdin for vengeance, and you for the security of his kingdom. He hardly cares about Sinbad, who is a mere pawn in this game of power." She frowned. "He wants you both dead."

"Yes, of course," Duban agreed. "And we would prefer to have Zeyn dead, or as close to it as an immortal could come. So we understand each other."

"Better than you and I understand each other," I said. "How can you even consider walking into that dragon trap?"

Duban almost smiled. "It's worse. We need Jewel Nymph there too."

"Me!" Nylon squealed, so much like Jewel that I almost laughed. "If Zeyn ever got me into his castle he would bind me naked on a table with my legs wide apart and my mouth blocked open and put his minions into continuous rape duty before he plucked out my eyeballs and cut out my heart with a trowel. Then he would ponder ways to torture me."

Duban was perplexed. "Why would he prop your mouth open? So you could better scream?"

"So I couldn't bite."

"But if you were tied down, you couldn't get at anyone to bite."

"Oh, I could, and would. The moment one of them—"

"Never mind," I said, not wanting to expose my son to the detail of the adult activity to which she referred. Then I had my own question: "You have a heart?"

"Only an emulation of one, while I remain immortal. But he would dig into my flesh for the sake of the mutilation. To make me ugly, and thus humiliate me. He could not hurt me physically, of course, as my gouged organs would quickly regenerate, but the indignity would be appalling. It would become burdensome in the course of centuries."

Centuries of torture. Just so. "So why do you want her there too?" I asked Duban.

"So she could emulate me while standing athwart the portal to Hades."

"How do you know of that?" Nylon demanded.

Now Duban squeezed Myrrh's arm. "My girlfriend would do anything to please me. She pleases me by providing information. Even some she shouldn't. She can't help herself, when I really want it." He looked at me, as Myrrh looked suitably guilty. "The portal is just within the castle, unknown to Prince Zeyn. We need to get safely into the castle to gain access to it."

So he was using the Myrrh Nymph for his own purposes. He did have a cunning mind. He had picked up on my idea to have a Nubile Nymph emulate him by such a portal. I realized that the ploy just might work. If Zeyn thought we were escaping, and he caught us, he would pounce on Duban without much caution. But this was fraught with dangerous complications. "Exactly where inside the castle?" I asked. "How could it be there, and Zeyn not find it?"

"Where Zeyn never thought to look," Nylon replied. "In the servant's privy. It is ill-kept and it smells, but they have no choice but to use it. They have no idea of its significance, as the portal is invisible and inoperative until invoked. Only we know of it, and that information has been useless to us. Even if we were captive in that ill castle and wanted to escape, we would not indulge in a one-way trip to Hades. No one would."

"But if Zeyn were to pounce into it, unknowing…" I said, considering the ramifications with growing interest.

"He would be gone, and we would be safe," Duban concluded. "His minions might be annoyed, but I could handle them, in the absence of Zeyn. That evens up the odds."

"It does indeed," I agreed. "But you know, there's many a slip twist the chalice and the lip. This is so chancy that only a fool would even consider it."

"Or someone desperate to save a friend, however unworthy that friend might be."

"What do you think?" I asked Nylon. "Would you care to risk such an insane venture?"

"Well, it would not be boring," she said. That was her way of saying yes. She had explained to us how boring immortality was. But was that her only motive?

That made me think: suppose Jewel and Myrrh, trying to recover the Lamp, fell into evil clutches and died? What would there be for Duban and me? Myrrh Nymph and Jewel Nymph. We might find it necessary to go the way Sinbad had, into denial leading to a new reality. The Nymphs would see to it that we never regretted that choice.

And, of course, Nylon did want to save her daughter. So it did all add up. I was sure we could trust her, regardless; I just liked to be certain things made sense.

The Nymphs' motive was not hostile, and we did need their help. So it was best not to look this gift camel too closely in the mouth.

"Then it seems we are decided," I said more briskly than I felt. "We will proffer a trade of hostages. But how can we be sure Zeyn will honor his side of the deal?"

"That is the beauty of integrity," Nylon said. "He must release them first. Then we will go to his castle. He is dishonest as the day is long, and days can be extremely long in Djinnland, but he knows you will honor your part of the deal. So we don't need to trust him; he will trust you."

"But I've often lied," I protested. "Sometimes it's good business practice."

"But have you ever reneged on a formal commitment?"

"No, of course not."

"And only the broad agreement will be formal," she continued. "Let Sinbad go; you and Duban will report to his front gate. All else is vague. He will be so eager he won't even consider that it might be a counter-trap."

"But I thought you were coming too."

"I am. My daughter is, too."

I shook my head, confused.

"As rings," she explained gently. "No need to inform Zeyn of that minor detail. Not that he would object; he would welcome the chance to capture two more Nubile Nymphs for his entertainment."

Entertainment: centuries of rape and torture of beautiful women. I shuddered.

Duban was nodding as she spoke. He had known it all along. Once again I was the dull one out.

Still, I had more objections. "Suppose he beheads us right there? Or chains us, or locks us in a steel chest?"

"He may," Duban said. "My magical powers do not match his, here in Djinnland, but they are not inconsequential. I will conjure us elsewhere in the castle. So we will have honored our commitment, but will still be free to act. He will have to run us down, which he should enjoy, cat and mouse."

"And we will head for the privy," Nylon said. "Where you will remove your rings and we'll assume the likenesses of what Zeyn most desires to see: you and Duban, ripe for capture and execution."

"Hiding in the servant's stinking privy," Duban continued. "Where he will wrinkle his nose and pounce without thinking."

"And go to Hades," Myrrh Nymph concluded.

Thus catching Zeyn in the same kind of trap that he had caught us in, portaling us to Djinnland. It seemed almost too pat. Things were bound to go wrong. They always did. But what else was there?

"We'll do it," I said more gamely than I felt.

120

CHAPTER TWENTY-FOUR

We waited only a short while before a messenger appeared at the portal.

Prior to that, I had been nervously lounging with Nymph Jewel in her spacious lodge, while Duban practiced his magic with one of the elder Nymphs. Through a window, I watched him quickly master what I could only imagine were very intricate spells. Glowing dragons appeared and disappeared. The elder Nymph herself grew suddenly to a great height, and then shrank so small that Duban held her upon the flat of his hand. They both laughed.

"Your son is powerful," said Nymph Jewel, looking out the window. "I can see why Prince Zeyn fears him."

I nodded absently, too nervous to think of anything other than my friend. I paced before the great hearth, as the hellbeast snapped playfully at my heels.

"Relax, my king," said Nylon. "We will hear from Zeyn soon. He has no need to keep your friend and my daughter longer than need be."

"Which is what makes me nervous. What if he kills them?"

"Zeyn has never been one to kill anyone too quickly. And besides, they are of more use to him alive than dead."

A young Nymph suddenly appeared in the doorway of the lodge. "My Queen, a messenger has arrived at the portal. He is alone and unarmed. He brings word from Prince Zeyn."

"Show him in."

Moments later, a young djinn manifested in the lodge. He smiled pleasantly and bowed deeply to both the queen and to myself. "My King and Queen, Prince Zeyn sends his deepest regrets to the senseless attack on your daughter, Nydea, and on your friend, Sinbad. The rogue worm has, of course, been captured and slaughtered and Nydea and Sinbad have been mercifully saved. For now, they are residing comfortably in Prince Zeyn's castle—"

"Out with it, demon," snapped Queen Nylon. "We do not have all day."

Immediately, the pleasant-looking djinn turned into something rather nasty. Now, a misshapen creature with an elongated head and glowing red eyes stood before us.

"Ye*sss*," hissed the foul creature. "They are in the prince's castle where they are no doubt being tortured at thi*ss* very moment."

"And what does the Prince want in exchange for their lives?"

"It i*sss* easy enough, my queen. He simply require*sss* an exchange."

"What kind of exchange?"

"The king and the boy, and you will have your fair daughter again, and the worthless *sss*ailor. They appear to be in love, after all." And the demon actually spat the word *love*.

Nylon and I had already gone over this moment, and she put on a wonderful show of being infuriated with the demands of Prince Zeyn. The demon only watched her with eager, round eyes, dripping its foul poison. Finally, in accordance with our rehearsed plan, I reached out a hand and took her arm.

"Duban and I will do it," I said.

"No, my king. I cannot allow—"

"We will do it." And here I looked at the demon. "For true love."

The demon actually seemed to fight an urge to vomit. When the creature got control of itself, it finally said, "Good, good. The Prince will be very plea*sss*sed."

"On one condition," I said.

The demon turned its full—and frightening—gaze on to me. I did my best not to look too deeply into its red eyes. "And what isss that, King Aladdin?"

"That he releases Sinbad and Nydea first."

"Oh, I don't think my massster will be pleased with that at all."

"It is my only condition. He can accept it or shove it up his fat ass."

The demon sized me up, its deformed head swiveling slightly on its long neck. "And what guarantee doesss the Prince have that King Aladdin will follow through on hisss end of the deal?"

"Because," I said, and this time I did look the vile creature full in the face, "King Aladdin never reneges on his word."

The demon continued staring at me, and I could not help but notice that the red in his eyes could have been actual fire, burning just behind its pupils.

Finally the demon began to nod. "Thisss is acceptable to the prince."

The demon obviously had been authorized to accept such a deal, as I doubted the creature could be in contact with the Prince in the Nymph's safe haven.

"Good," I said. "When my friends are here, safe and sound, my son and I will present ourselves outside the castle walls."

"Thisss, too, is acceptable."

Nymph Jewel stood suddenly. "Then begone, foul creature."

It bowed and disappeared into a puff of black smoke. I had barely returned to Nymph Jewel's side, when the same young Nymph appeared again in the doorway.

"My Queen, Sinbad the Sailor and Nydea are at the portal."

———

We were all gathered around the central fire of the lodge. Sinbad hated our plan, but I reminded him that I had given the Prince my word.

"Your word, be damned, King Aladdin. The man is a devil. He was all set to torture us. In fact, I had already been stretched over a heavily scarred table stained with blood. Next to me was all manner of torture devices, all stained with fresh blood." Sinbad stepped in front of me, his wild eyes aflame. "This camel turd does not deserve respect or any man's word."

"We have a plan," said Queen Nylon.

"With all due respect, your plan is foolish, my queen. Perhaps the most foolish I have ever heard."

The Queen cocked an eyebrow. "Oh? More foolish than venturing deep into the Siren's enchanted cavern?"

"Well, that was a different—"

I clapped a hand on Sinbad's shoulder. "My friend," I said, "if I have learned anything from my time as king it is that sometimes there is a time to fight. And now is such a time. Prince Zeyn is determined to not only destroy me, but my son. If he succeeds he will usher in, from all appearance, a reign of terror the likes of which our world has never seen before."

"And so your great plan to stop him is to simply give yourselves up?"

"I never said it was great. But it is a plan."

"I'm coming with you."

"No—"

"You will need a second sword, Aladdin. I have seen the inside of his palace and it is frightening to behold. The very walls themselves are embedded with an army of stone demons."

Duban spoke up. "I can just as easily turn him into a ring, Father."

"I'm running out of fingers," I grumbled. But I appeared to be outnumbered. Nylon had no opinion in the matter, apparently, and who was I to keep my adventurous friend from helping me? "Fine. Then let's get on with it."

"My Queen," said the same young Nymph. "The demon awaits at the portal to transport King Aladdin and Prince Duban."

Nymph Jewel nodded. "Indeed. Let's get on with it. Duban, work your magic."

My stepson did just that, quickly turning Nymph Jewel, Nymph Myrrh and Sindbad the Sailor into golden rings, all of which I placed on various fingers. I remembered how when I had become a ring, it was mere brass. Not that I was jealous, exactly, merely off put.

I turned to the young Nymph. "Now, take us to the demon."

CHAPTER TWENTY-FIVE

All too soon we were at the portal, then in the underground passage, rejoining the demon, who grinned horrendously and ushered us into his carriage. What was odd was that it appeared to be a very nice carriage, with plush upholstery, tasteful curtains to shield us from dust, and soft cushions on the bench. We were quite comfortable.

The demon then became a four legged beast that stepped into a harness and hauled the carriage forward. Right out of the passage and into the ground, for all of it was of mortal density, making the ground seem like fog. Zeyn had had time to prepare for our density. We cruised on along the bedrock and upward toward the surface.

By mutual consent we did not discuss our strategy, but kept our words innocuous. We were able to converse freely in the carriage. "Prince Zeyn is being a remarkably gracious host," I remarked.

"I'm sure he can be that, when he chooses," Duban said, grimacing. He shrugged. "Possibly we have misjudged the Prince."

I forced a straight face. "Possibly, though my prior encounter with him might be construed as a bit negative."

"Maybe he happened to be in a bad mood that day," Duban said, quirking a smile. After all, he had had his own negative experience with Zeyn, who had sought to sacrifice him on an altar.

We drew up to the surface. Then the carriage sprouted wings and flew off the ground and into the sky. That was impressive, considering our phenomenal density.

The high turrets of the dread castle came into view. The thing was amazingly aesthetic, resembling a storybook residence. I was surprised.

"Illusion," Duban murmured.

Oh. Of course. Very little here in Djinnland needed to be as it appeared.

I thought of something else. "We are mortally dense. How can any of us go above the bedrock level of the castle?"

"Prince Zeyn surely thought of that detail," Duban said. "The castle must be enchanted to handle mortal density. Sinbad did not have any trouble."

That was true. Outside the castle our density counted, but inside it we might very well seem normal. Just as we did here in the carriage.

We landed in a central courtyard. Two pretty maidens were there to welcome us, each more comely than the other. They were tastefully clothed in light robes and sashes that did nothing to conceal their shapeliness. "Welcome, honored guests!" the loveliest one exclaimed, stepping forward to give me a kiss, while the other bussed Duban. I managed not to stiffen in alarm. "I am Desiree, and my companion is Demona, both of us dedicated to serve you." She smiled and made a little flirt of her hips and long loose dark hair. "In any manner you may desire, pun intended."

I got it: Desiree, desire.

What theater, Nylon thought, disgusted.

She's really a warty pig? I inquired.

No, her physical appearance is accurate, and I'm sure she is more than ready to oblige your manly passion, having densified so that she can. But she's a demoness who would consume you if allowed.

I saw nothing like this before, Sinbad grumped, now having access to my thoughts, as well.

Just so. Since it was not incidental demonesses we were after, I had to play along. Only when Zeyn showed up to make his move would we make our break. We needed to have him chasing us, so that we could lead him into the trap.

"This way, please, King Aladdin," Desiree said, taking my hand while Demona took Duban's hand. They conducted us to an elaborate suite replete with fountains and works of art. Stone statues lined the walls. Demonic statues, all armed with stone swords. Zeyn's army. There was a great golden throne that sat empty nearby. I had a strong feeling this was where Zeyn was entertained. Were we to be his entertainment? I shivered.

Demona spoke next, "You must be tired and worn after your journey, not to mention suffering the nefarious attentions of the Nasty Nymphs. We will be happy to help you bathe and change."

What was going on here? We had been braced for attack and torture. Zeyn had no need to coddle us. "We can handle such details ourselves," I said gruffly.

"Of course, King Aladdin," she agreed immediately. "Make yourselves comfortable. We will bring you your repast."

Did they plan to drug us with bhang in the food? Again, why should Zeyn bother? We were already in his power. This simply was not making much sense.

I am baffled too, Nylon thought.

They brought a veritable banquet, which they served us piece by piece. Nylon and Sylvie, who evidently knew something about poison, assured me that the food was safe and of excellent quality. This was strange, as djinn and demons did not really need to eat. Zeyn maintained a kitchen to serve mortals?

"Prince Zeyn has provided also for your entertainment," Desiree said. Before I could protest that Duban did not need a woman, and I would not indulge in his presence regardless, she gestured. The wall facing us changed color, becoming what seemed to be a window. We saw through it to a harbor with a ship. "A window to the mortal realm."

In fact it was the harbor at Cloudland Island, and the Fat Chance. And there aboard it were three people: a handsome man, a lovely woman, and a pretty girl.

"Mother!" Duban breathed. "Myrrh!"

"And surely the Thief of Baghdad," I concluded somewhat sourly. "So they made it to the ship. But did they get the Lamp?"

"Mother is carrying it," Duban said.

So she was, in a little handbag. So they had arrived in time, while Zeyn was distracted with us. "But I think they need to get away from there," I muttered. "Soon."

"Also, she got new shoes," Duban said distastefully. "The Thief must have gotten them for her."

"They are pretty slippers," I agreed. Trust my wife to keep her eye out for shoes, even amidst serious business. She also had fancy gloves. I shook my head with fond bemusement.

But before they could board the Thief's carpet, three men arrived. "Aladdin!" Jewel exclaimed. "You got free!" She ran to gladly embrace him.

But of course it was not Aladdin. I was right here in Zeyn's castle, watching this travesty. The others looked like Sinbad and Duban, and I was pretty sure they weren't authentic either.

"We did," the impostor agreed. "It is quite a story, which we will tell at another time. Prince Zeyn is hot on our trail, breathing fire. Your carpet won't hold six people. We need Ifrit Iften. Give me the Lamp."

"Don't do it!" I protested, but of course she couldn't hear me. The magic window enabled us to hear them, but not vice versa. I was coming to appreciate the nature of Zeyn's torture of us: to see disaster happening and be powerless to prevent it.

"Of course, dear," Jewel said. She brought the lamp out and proffered it. Ouch!

Zeyn—for it had to be he—snatched it from her hand. He held it up and rubbed its side. "Come forth, O Iften!" he intoned. "Now you are mine, ifrit, and must serve me!"

Purple smoke issued from the Lamp. Also, evidently, a vile odor. Zeyn and his companions coughed and squinched their tearing eyes shut.

If I didn't know better, Nylon thought, *I'd figure that to be a stink bomb.*

It is *a stink bomb!* Sylvie Siren thought. *The Thief stole several from our treasure. It emits a truly putrid stench admixed with mustard gas, a substance from the foul future.*

"Then she saw him coming!" I said, gratified as well as amused. "But then why did she hug him?"

She planted something on him, Sylvie thought. *It looked like another stolen artifact, a homing signal.*

"So she will know him wherever he goes, whatever form he assumes," I said. "That's my girl."

Duban looked at me. "There is something?"

Quickly I explained the dialogue with the rings. He smiled. "That's mother," he agreed. "Myrrh would have anticipated this ploy when she read the future, and then read his mind, so they were never fooled."

"But they're still in deadly danger," I said. "They need to get out of there *now.*"

Indeed, they were doing so. While Zeyn and his henchmen coughed, choked, and rubbed their stinging eyes, Jewel, Myrrh, and the Thief were retreating to their magic carpet. They got on it and took off.

But then Zeyn's two minions transformed to winged monsters and flew to intercept the trio. Their eyes no longer flowed; in this form they were immune. In fact they were probably made from stink bomb ingredients. Meanwhile Zeyn also shed his mortal mask and stood revealed as himself, no longer coughing. "Fetch them back here," he ordered.

The two monsters took hold of the carpet, and it was helpless against their strength. They dragged it back down before Zeyn. The ploy had failed.

"You will pay for this little trick, wench," Zeyn said grimly. "But I will spare you if you give me the real Lamp. Where is it?"

"I'll never tell," Jewel said.

"You *will* tell," he told her. "Because I have your husband hostage in my castle, and I will torture him in your presence until his screams make you yield. You can save him some pain by producing the Lamp now."

"Never!" she said bravely. "And you'll never find it!"

A crocodile would have admired his smile. "I hoped you would say that, strumpet. Now I have an excellent pretext to torture him and the boy, and of course part of it will be them seeming me rape you and the girl child, before I turn you over to my lustful minions. I will of course still recover the Lamp after our frolics. This will surely be a wonderful occasion."

"You monster!" she said fervently, and Myrrh looked horrified.

"Indeed," he agreed equably.

I shook my head. They had after all walked into the trap. Now Prince Zeyn had us all, and he would be merciless.

Yet if Myrrh could read minds and see the future, how could this have happened?

"They're up to something," Duban murmured.

They certainly are, Nylon thought.

They're women, Sylvie agreed. *The girl faked horror very nicely.*

They mean to rescue their beloveds, Nydea Nymph thought. *The Lamp was just a pretext.*

I hoped they were right, because I couldn't see any chance. I worried they had underestimated Zeyn's power in his home castle. I feared we were all doomed.

CHAPTER TWENTY-SIX

I watched in horror as Zeyn's minions surrounded Jewel, Myrrh and the Thief. Zeyn then turned and looked directly at us. A shiver ran through me. Even Duban gasped. Zeyn's dark eyes flared briefly with amusement, then turned sinister as his eyebrows drew together. He raised his hands and snapped his fingers, and the wall before us went blank, replaced now by bricks and tapestries.

Duban took my hand. "They're here, Father."

"Who?" I said.

"Myrrh and mother. The thief, too." Duban closed his eyes. "Myrrh's reaching out to me...they're in a dungeon, deep below the castle."

That's where he had me strapped to the torture table, came Sinbad's thoughts.

Sinbad's words had just appeared in my thoughts when a brilliant flash of light appeared in the great hall. The air in the room seemed to drop many degrees. When my seared eyes could focus again, I was not too surprised to see the hulking figure of Prince Zeyn slouching on the golden throne.

Coldness radiated from the prince. Indeed, as he breathed, small puffs of condensation billowed around him. What manner of foul creature was he?

The foulest, thought Nylon, squeezing my finger. *In Djinnland, cold of heart also translates into cold of flesh. He is the prodigy of two powerful magicians. His father was a great mortal wizard and his mother the most powerful of djinn sorceresses. Zeyn, of course, destroyed them both as soon as he grew powerful enough. Now, he forever longs to rule both worlds.*

"So we meet again, boy," said Zeyn. He motioned with his hand and sexy female slaves appeared instantly by his side. Whether they were djinn, mortals or demons, I had no idea.

Kidnapped mortals, thought Sylvie. *Their memories have been erased. They serve only to pleasure the prince. When he is tired of them, they will be given to others who have shown Zeyn loyalty. Generally, they live only as long as their beauty holds.*

Zeyn was sounding worse and worse. Then again, what else did I expect? The world is full of a long list of rulers who abused their power. Apparently, Djinnland was no different. I hoped to break the cycle.

Duban stepped bravely forward. Bravely, because I could see his small shoulders shaking. "You have my mother. I want her released. Additionally, I want all of us released or you will be destroyed. This is your only warning."

Zeyn, who had been absently patting the behind of a dark-haired slave girl, threw back his head and laughed. The slaves all laughed nervously. Their faces, I saw were completely blank. Mere shells.

"We are not in the mortal realm, boy," said Zeyn, resuming his patting. "Your magic is insufficient here. Ah, but I admire your spirit, which, of course, I shall break soon enough."

Desiree stepped forward and bowed, and only then did I see something sticking down below her tunic. A forked tale that seemed to have a mind of its own, as it slithered and curled in mid-air. "Sire," she said. "King Aladdin has with him two Nymphs, a Siren and Sinbad the Sailor. I knew this the moment I took his hand."

"Oh, how is this so?" His scanning eyes, which sat behind thick folds of fat, spotted the rings. "Ah, you are a fashionable king, I see."

He snapped his fingers and instantly all four rings sprang from my fingers. The rings shot through the air, to land lightly within his open palm. He looked at them curiously, then started nodding.

"A fine bit of magic," he said, then began placing each ring onto his own hands. The rings, I saw, magically fit the size of any fingers, since his were easily twice as thick as my own. "There. Now I can be fashionable, too. And also safeguard myself against any mischief you might have had in mind, King Aladdin. Wherever I go, these rings go with me."

My heart sank. This was surely not going to plan. "Release them," I said. "You have no need for them."

"No need for three sexy vixens...and a mortal male who bleeds so readily? Surely you jest!" Zeyn rubbed the rings salaciously, then threw his head back and guffawed. "I see our friend Sinbad has quite the salty mouth on him. Well, we will see how much fight he has in him soon enough."

Zeyn waved his hand and two of the stone creatures directly behind us stepped away from the wall. As they did so, I looked at Duban. "Now."

Just as I felt a heavy hand drop onto my shoulder, the boy snapped his own fingers and suddenly we were elsewhere.

Behind me still stood the stone demon, but now we were alone in a dank hallway, surrounded by metal doors and bars, and the cries and screams of those in deep agony.

The stone demon raised its sword and I acted instinctively, unleashing a punch straight to the foul creature's turgid face. The pain in my hand was nearly unbearable. I recoiled, crying out. Duban stepped forward, raising both his hands, and the stone stature crumbled in a heap of broken rock.

My step-son looked up at me sadly. "Really, father? Punching a stone statue?"

I held my punched hand against me, certain I had broken a knuckle or two. From the torches, the screaming and the steady sounds of dripping water, I knew we were in the dungeon.

"Let's get out of here," I said.

Duban pointed behind me. "Myrrh's telling me they're that way."

"Then let's go," I said, and we moved quickly through the twisting corridors, past closed doors, where pale faces and hands appeared in small windows, all beseeching us to help them. As difficult as it was to ignore those in need, we pushed forward. As a ruler, I was, of course not immune to dungeons. After all, below my very palace was such a bleak place. But I saw myself as a fair king and I did not enjoy torture for the sake of torture. Only the most hardened criminals found themselves in my dungeons, and even then they were treated far better than they deserved.

We passed a room with a sloping floor that led to a black water pit. Where the pit led off to, I didn't know, but I logged it away. Perhaps it would be a means of escape.

We rounded a corner and Duban pointed at another door. "They're in there," he said.

Indeed, as we drew close a welcomed sight appeared in the small window. Jewel's lovely face. My heart rammed in my chest, but as I moved toward her another face appeared—that of the handsome thief. He gave me a crooked, swarthy smile. I hated him already.

"King Aladdin," he said, nodding slightly. "If you're here to rescue us, you're going to need a fair bit of magic. These dungeon doors are enchanted. Even I can't break free."

"Stand back, father," said Duban. I noted that he did not tell the Thief of Baghdad to step back.

Duban raised his hands and intoned something just under his breath. Within moments the door sprang open.

Jewel dashed out and threw herself into my arms, as did little Myrrh into Duban's arms. The Thief of Baghdad watched all of us with a bemused smile.

"Now, who do I get to hug?" he asked jovially.

"Never mind that," I said, perhaps sharper than I should have, and I caught them all up to date.

"So what do we do next?" asked Jewel.

"We have a plan to destroy Zeyn once and for all."

"Except the pieces of your plan are currently wrapped around that fat bastard's fingers," said the Thief. "Myrrh read your mind as it happened, and told us the bad news."

He had a point. Myrrh looked at all of us. "I have an idea," she said.

CHAPTER TWENTY-SEVEN

I heard the heavy tramping of approaching feet. "It better be a good one," I said grimly. "Because that sounds like Prince Zeyn coming to collect us."

"It is that Jewel should invoke the lyre," Myrrh said. "For Duban to play for the monsters and demons."

Jewel nodded, smiling wickedly. "That will do," she said.

"Mother, you know how I love music," Duban said. "But I would not care to entertain the deadly minions of this fell castle. In any event, we have serious business afoot, such as saving our lives."

Prince Zeyn rounded a corner, leading a small army of horrendously ugly creatures. "I could hardly have put it better myself. But let's humor the lady. Where is this musical instrument? I see none on her."

"Because you haven't looked closely dirt-face," Jewel said. She lifted her left knee high enough to provide me a compelling glimpse of her thigh and buttock, and removed her slipper. "lyre, restore."

The slipper expanded. In a moment it was a beautiful translucent, jewel-encrusted lyre, surely another valuable item the Thief had stolen from the cache of the Sirens. She handed it to Duban.

Duban took it, though his mouth was opening for another protest. Then he paused, fondling it as he glanced at Myrrh. She was evidently telling him something mentally. "Oh, my! It's magic!"

"Oh, my indeed," Zeyn said. "I recognize that device. It is the infamous Lucent Lyre, reputed to glow when expertly played, and to be a favorite of monsters and demons. It has been out of circulation for several centuries; interesting that it should turn up now. Surely an excellent choice, if you have the talent. But it will burn the fingers of anyone who attempts to play it inexpertly." His lips twitched cruelly. "Play it, boy; we'll wait on your performance."

I stifled my anger. Zeyn thought Duban was a novice. He had a surprise coming.

"Thank you," Duban said. His fingers stroked the strings. Then he played.

The music was lovely. The lyre did glow, brightening as the boy got into the melody. There was no sign of fingers burning as the music spread out to fill the dungeon.

Then there was another sound. A kind of thudding, as of many feet striking the stone floor simultaneously. It came from behind Zeyn. I looked.

The monsters were dancing. All of them, in unison, their feet striking the floor in intricate patterns governed by the music. It was weird, because they were hardly the dancing type. They clearly were not good at it, but were compelled by the music.

"So it's true!" Zeyn said, amazed. "It does make monsters dance! I thought that an exaggeration. I am impressed; you do have musical talent, boy." He frowned. "Now desist; we need to talk."

"We have nothing to talk about," Duban said. "Your monsters can not serve you as long as I am playing. The ones in the walls, too; they will dance until they shake the castle down. I suggest you vacate the premises before the walls start collapsing."

Indeed, the whole castle seemed to be vibrating with increasing force. I am not normally claustrophobic, but this made me uneasy. We could all be crushed by falling rock.

"Desist, or I will punish your associates," Zeyn said. "Beginning with your friend, Sinbad the Sailor, who is now in my power." He touched the Sinbad ring.

Duban paused, focusing. The monsters halted their dancing, abruptly frozen in place. Then he played an odd chord.

Zeyn grimaced. "The rings are burning!" he exclaimed. He wrenched them off his fingers.

All four rings dropped to the floor, reverting to their original forms as they did. Suddenly there stood Sinbad the Sailor, Sylvie Siren, Queen Nylon Nymph and Nydea Nymph. They quickly stepped away from Zeyn.

"I am not an entire idiot about magic," Duban said. "I made those rings; I control them regardless who wears them. I'm surprised you forgot that detail."

"I merely misjudged your power to perform such magic in my castle," Zeyn said thoughtfully. "You have grown, Duban."

"I have an issue to settle with you," Duban said. "You tried to murder me last year. Did you think I would enter your stronghold unprepared? Your magic may still be stronger than mine, here in Djinnland, but you have allowed me to bypass your defenses and cut off your allies. Just as a maiden may kill a warrior, if she catches him unaware, I have seized the advantage over you in this spot locale. Do you care to try my strength now?" His fingers quivered over the lyre, which continued to glow though it was not being played at the moment. It seemed to be responding to the power of the one who held it.

"Not at the moment," Zeyn said. He did not look cowed or even nervous. That made *me* nervous. "As I said, it is time to talk."

"What could you possibly have to say that any of us would want to hear?" Sinbad demanded. "We want you dead and forgotten."

"Hear me out," Zeyn said. "I have an offer to make to you, severally and individually."

"Don't listen to him," the Thief said. "He's a bigger thief than I am, because he has no conscience."

Zeyn turned to him. "You have a talent I can use. Swear fealty to me and I will give you Desiree Demoness to be your slave, mistress, or wife." He gestured and Desiree appeared, phenomenally lovely in an exposive gown, smiling at the Thief. She inhaled, and I could see that the Thief was mightily impressed. The demoness fairly radiated sex appeal.

Zeyn turned to Duban. "I will give you the key to Musica, the land of music, where every instrument is magic. It is the origin of the Lucent Lyre. Every instrument there is similarly magical, capable of marvelously lovely music and magic. It is a land of peace; the inhabitants have no interest other than perfecting their music. With your talent you could make music such as you never could in the mortal realm. You can take Myrrh and she can learn an instrument too. You can find fulfillment there."

Duban's expression softened. This interested him.

"Ridiculous!" Jewel said sharply. "Only a fool would even consider such nonsense."

Zeyn focused on her. "You are a truly beautiful and spirited woman, well fit to be a queen. Why settle for an indifferent character like Aladdin, who achieved his crown mainly because he had the luck to get hold of the Lamp, when you could become queen of Djinnland *and* the mortal realm? Marry me, and you will be that."

Jewel's mouth worked for a moment before she could speak. "What unearthly arrogance makes you think I would ever touch *you*, you fell monster?"

Zeyn smiled. "Why, I don't know. Perhaps it was that flash of thigh you showed when you produced the Lyre. Your leg is as lovely as the rest of you, numbing my more sensible nature. It makes me desire you passionately."

"I'm pregnant!" she snapped.

"For the moment," he agreed.

What griped me was that she was proffering a reason for him not to want her, rather than hurling his offer back in his face. Was the evil lord making an impression on her? "And what of me?" I asked.

"Give me the Lamp, and you can marry queen Nylon and be rapturously happy while governing a kingdom consisting of nothing but lovely Nubile Nymphs."

"As if he would ever consider that," Sinbad said.

Zeyn turned to him. "You have no real business here. Return to the mortal realm with your wife, whom you purchased with the shipload of treasure. She will make you unspeakably happy."

Thus Zeyn was dealing with every one of us, in his fashion. But why was he bothering, knowing that none of us were likely to accept? For one thing, he wasn't trustworthy; even if the deals were good, we could not trust him to honor them.

I came to a preliminary conclusion: he was stalling for time. Duban had him with his scimitar down, and he needed to summon reinforcements. We could not afford to let them arrive.

CHAPTER TWENTY-EIGHT

Myrrh, I thought, *can you read Prince Zeyn's mind?*

Myrrh nodded and closed her eyes. Meanwhile, Duban had stopped playing and the demons had stopped dancing. From having fought battles before, I sensed the enemy surrounding us on both sides. We were not in a good position.

No, my king, came the girl's words. *He has shielded his mind.*

Now I sensed movement behind me, and I could see now what Zeyn had been stalling for. It was another army, but this one was different. Oddly lumbering. Dripping water, their clothing in tatters, I vaguely recognized some of them from the whirpool islands. Zombies. I didn't have the all the facts, but I suspected they emerged from the water pit we had seen earlier, a sinkhole that somehow magically connected to Zombie Island.

"I believe you've met my friends," said Prince Zeyn. "And as luck would have it, they're also immune to the magic of the lyre. Unfortunately for you, they have a hunger for human brain. Why a zombie needs brains is beyond me, but I don't make the rules. On second thought, Aladdin, I withdraw my offer."

The undead continued toward us, many dragging badly damaged limbs, and some even pulling their legless, decomposed bodies with bony hands. The clickety-clack of bone striking the stone floor filled the tunnel, as did the zombies themselves. There were hundreds of them, if not thousands, stretching as far down the tunnel as the wavering torchlight would reveal.

Myrrh whimpered next to me. I didn't blame her. I put an arm around her.

"I guess we might need these," said Jewel, and she raised her hands and both gloves turned into swords. The swords glowed with an inner light. Magical swords, perhaps impervious to breaking. No doubt stolen by the Thief.

She tossed one to the scoundrel, who caught it easily, swiped it expertly in the air and held it out before him. Sinbad next drew his scimitar, as wooden staffs appeared in the hands of the Nymphs. Sylvie the Siren lifted her own hand and a blazing pitchfork appeared.

So this was it. Demons on one side and zombies on the other, and we had, what, three swords, two staffs and a pitchfork?

We were doomed.

I'd been in some tough scraps before, some of which appeared nearly hopeless. But this clearly topped them all. For the first time in my storied life, I was truly without hope and without ideas.

It was time to fight to the bitter end.

"I shall take that," said Zeyn, and he snapped his fingers and Duban's lyre flew from his hands to crumple against the far wall.

And that's when the demons charged on one side, and the zombies from the other. Our little group formed a circle, our backs to each other, our weapons out, the children in the middle, and as the horde from Hades bore down on us, my wife did a most curious thing.

She raised her foot and removed her final slipper.

Which, in turned, formed into a golden lamp. It had been hidden on her all along. Cunning woman!

"Lamprey!" I yelled.

Just then Duban stepped forward and raised his hands as something sparked off of an invisible barrier—no doubt the prince's attempt to summon the lamp. The boy had protected us. I seized the lamp and rubbed it quickly.

Smoke billowed out, and soon Lamprey's tall, ethereal form appeared in the air before us. He bowed toward me.

"Help us, Lamprey!" I cried.

"Your wish is my—"

"Just do it!"

He bowed again and in an instant the demons were blown off their feet. Likewise, the zombies were hurled backward. Prince Zeyn shrieked with rage and grew rapidly in size. Now standing in his place was a massive minotaur, with the body of a man and the head of a bull. Its nostrils flared and steam issued out as it charged our group. Lamprey instantly transformed as well, in like size and shape, and met the charging minotaur head-on. There was thunderous clash of horns. Both minotaurs rebounded, stunned.

"C'mon!" yelled the Thief of Baghdad, and he dashed off through the tunnel, now lined with fallen demons. And like the true scoundrel that he was, he never bothered to look back. Whether we followed or not was obviously no concern of his. I took Duban's hand and Jewel took Myrrh's, and together the rest of us followed behind a charred path of toasted demons.

We soon found a curving flight of stairs and headed up, and shortly we were in the castle proper. Here, many gaping holes revealed where the demons had stepped forth. The floor shook as thunderous explosions issued up from the subterranean tunnels where the two powerful djinni locked horns.

"Where to now?" asked Jewel.

The Thief of Baghdad was nowhere to be found. The worthless dog had no doubt fled the castle. To where, I hadn't a clue, and I gave the man no further thought. Meanwhile, the very castle itself continued to shake and rattle as the beastly minotaurs continued bashing heads down below.

"They will battle to the end, and one will die," said Nylon, who had now reverted to looking like my dead wife. I saw the reason why: Jewel herself was here. What good was a replica when the real deal was nearby? As she spoke, Nylon touched my arm in an overly familiar way. Jewel caught the Nymph's intimate gesture and raised an eyebrow. I shrugged Nylon's hand off me and idly wondered how the Nymph Queen appeared to Jewel. No doubt her magical charm was lost on the females of our race.

Still, I understood Nylon's meaning. Now fully recovered, Lamprey was surely as powerful as Prince Zeyn, but there was no guarantee that my djinn would come out of this victorious.

"But I have no control over my djinn," I said. "I commanded his help, but he could have just as easily refused. We are in the land of djinn, after all, where my authority over him is moot."

Nylon was shaking her head. "Their battle goes beyond you, King Aladdin. Last year, Zeyn had gained the upper hand by trapping Ifrit Iften when your djinn had been in your service, and thus at a disadvantage. But now released, they will settle an old grudge."

"But I do not want Lamprey to perish."

"He may not. He may very well destroy the foul prince once and for all."

"Or not," I said.

"Or not," agreed Nylon. "Unless…"

"Unless what?"

"You call out for his help, and thus summon him away from Zeyn."

"I can do that," I agreed. "But what's the point, if my summoning distracts and weakens Lamprey?"

"Zeyn will give chase, and instead will find me, resembling young Duban. But I can only hold the deception for a short period."

I nodded, recalling our plan. "And you yourself will be standing at the portal to Hades?"

"Where that fat bastard will rot for all eternity."

"Now that," I said, "sounds like a plan."

CHAPTER TWENTY-NINE

I rubbed the lamp again. "Lamprey!" I called. "I need you!" Would he respond? We were counting on it.

He did, appearing in human form. "Aladdin, I am busy at the moment," he said urgently.

"I know it! But we have our own plan to deal with Zeyn. Hide yourself, and if our plan doesn't work out, then you can take him on again."

He shook his head as if bemused by dealing with foolish mortals. "I hardly think—"

"Humor me."

He sighed and faded out.

We forged on through the residential section of the castle, heading for the servants' quarters, and the servants' privy. But the castle was huge, and we soon got lost in its labyrinth. The demons were coming after us, and we had to chop at them constantly, cutting off limbs and snouts to keep them at bay.

Then the demons retreated. Apparently we had entered a section where they were were forbidden. What could it be?

We found ourselves in an apparent cul-de-sac, a storage area where an assortment of treasure items was piled. Gold, silver, diamonds, pearls, elaborate weapons, fancy clothing, bound dancing girls—all the usual.

And there was the Thief of Baghdad, busy sorting through it all, looking for the best things to steal. He hadn't even waited for the battle to finish.

Jewel was disgusted. "The man has his uses, but he's too damned shallow."

Then we heard the heavy tromping of hooves. "The minotaur!" Myrrh said. "Looking for Lamprey."

"Yes," Jewel agreed. "I'm tracking him by the sensor I planted on him."

I drew my scimitar. "Hide!" I told the others. "I'll take him on."

"You foolish man," Jewel said, almost fondly. "You can't hope to match his magic power."

"Let me handle this," Nylon said. "Hide, but keep your eyes locked on me." She glanced at Myrrh. "I will need your help. Keep your mind in touch." Myrrh nodded.

I wasn't sure what Nylon had in mind, but there wasn't time to argue. She needed me to watch her so she could emulate Jewel, my beloved, for others. Jewel and I hastily buried ourselves under invaluable embroidered carpets and peeked out to watch Nylon. Duban and Myrrh hid nearby. Sinbad and Nydea found their own hideout. I wasn't sure where Sylvie was. Only the Thief remained visible, oblivious to all but the treasures before him.

The minotaur appeared, snorting steam. Nylon, in the form of Jewel, spun about, as if discovering him unexpectedly. "Oh!" she cried, horrified.

"Haa!" he said. It seemed he could talk in this form if he chose to. "Come here, mortal tidbit!"

"Never!" She turned to flee.

He strode to catch her by her trailing hair. "Where is the fell ifrit? Tell me and I won't ravish you."

"Never!" she cried, struggling ineffectively. She lacked the sword Jewel had, not that it would have done her much good.

I kept my eyes locked on her, so that the illusion would not be broken.

He threw her down on the floor, holding her there by her hair. "I am not partial to this word 'never,' strumpet. Tell me!"

"I-I must not," she said, whimpering.

With his free hand he ripped off the front of her gown, exposing her torso from breasts to belly. "Last chance, slut. Tell me!"

I felt the real Jewel's hand clench in mine. This was too close to what she had experienced in the past.

Her resistance collapsed. "He—he's hiding in the servant's quarters, where he thinks you won't look."

"Excellent." The monster lowered his body onto hers.

"But you said you would not ravish me!" she protested tearfully.

"I lied." He thrust so savagely that her whole body slid along the floor. She screamed piercingly, from pain or outrage, but he did not relent. In a moment he had done it. "I doubt you are pregnant any more, after that plumbing, she-dog." Then he got up and forged on, leaving her sobbing on the floor.

"He thought that was me," Jewel murmured as we emerged from our hiding places. "That would have happened to me."

"Yes," I said tightly. "If he caught you alone."

Nylon got to her feet. "Of course he did not hurt me," she said, brushing herself off as her gown re-formed, intact. "I am invulnerable." She twitched a smile. "And not pregnant."

Jewel was clearly shaken. "I owe you one."

"Not yet," Nylon said. "We still need to eliminate Zeyn." She walked rapidly in the direction Zeyn had gone.

"She has to get to the portal before he does," Myrrh explained. She faced Jewel. "I had to tell her about the way you were raped in the past, so she could play the part. Now Zeyn is on his way to the servants' quarters, thanks to her."

"I really owe her," Jewel said.

"I need to get over there," Myrrh said. "To help her emulate Duban."

"I can fight my own battles!" Duban protested.

"If this works, you won't have to."

"But—"

She leaned forward quickly and kissed him. That completely shut him up. Then she hurried off.

"Women are like that," I advised him. "They run the show. But if our ploy fails, we will really be in for it, and you will need all your magic."

"We had better get over there," Duban said.

We hurried in the direction the others had gone. Soon we found the servant's quarters. Then Zeyn found us.

"I don't see Iften," he said. "Who should I torture next?"

"Me, you bag of garbage," Duban said. "If you have the gumption."

"Gumption!" Zeyn said outraged, and charged, horns down. But Duban was already moving out of the way. He ran into the next chamber, closely pursued by the minotaur.

We followed immediately after, uncertain what else to do. This seemed to be as much farce as combat. "We've got to stop that boy from getting himself killed," Jewel said.

There was the privy chamber. Duban was standing by the seat, balked by the walls of the enclosure. There was no escape.

"Tell me where Iften is," Zeyn said. "And maybe I won't turn you into a sausage and eat you."

"Eat your own foul guts!" Duban said. He raised his hands in a magical gesture.

Zeyn dived for him. And through him. The prince was gone without even a scream. He had of course never seen the trap coming, or he would have avoided it.

Duban's form wavered, becoming Queen Nylon, for a moment in her own form of a regal queen. "Got him," she said with satisfaction. "Thanks to Myrrh, who maintained her focus on me." Which had enabled her to emulate Myrrh's beloved, Duban.

Myrrh appeared. She hugged the Queen, who became a second Myrrh as Duban gazed at them.

"Thanks to *you!*" Jewel said. She hugged Nylon too, and they became two Jewels as I gazed at them.

"Thanks to us all," I said, highly gratified. Suddenly I was overcome with an emotion borne of relief. My vision clouded. No, of course I wasn't crying.

Jewel took my hand in hers. "Thanks mainly to your cunning plan," she said. "To trick him into that portal."

"Oh, Jewel, I'm so glad you weren't—"

She silenced me with a kiss. Then she led me to an adjacent chamber and pulled the curtain closed. She brought me to the bed and kissed me again, and pressed her wonderful body close to mine.

My passion for her exploded. Still, I demurred. "Jewel, you're—"

She kissed me again as she shrugged out of her gown. "One time won't hurt, beloved. As long as it's not too violent." She grimaced prettily, evidently thinking of the rape we had witnessed.

"No violence!" I agreed eagerly. With her I had no fear of impotence.

Soon we were in the throes of lovemaking. It was absolutely wonderful. "Oh, Jewel," I said as we relaxed. "I love you so much."

"There is something I should tell you," she said.

"Anything is fine with me, as long as I'm with you."

"It is not in my nature to deny you. But I'm not Jewel."

I stared at her. "I don't understand." But an awful notion was percolating through the thick mush of my brain. The two women had hugged, looking identical for a moment. Had I somehow gotten hold of the wrong one?

The curtain was pulled aside. "Aladdin, what are you up to?" the real Jewel demanded.

My world came crashing down around my shoulders. I had just cheated on my wife with the Queen of the Nubile Nymphs!

"You just couldn't wait to get into her pantaloons, could you!" Jewel said angrily. Not that Nylon had been wearing any such clothing. "The moment my back was turned! How could you!"

And what could I say in my defense? I had sinned badly.

Jewel came to touch Nylon, who still looked just like her. "And I'll bet he didn't give you any chance to get away. He just barreled in before you could explain."

"Well, not exactly. I was hardly unwilling."

Duban appeared. "You were cheating on Mother?" he asked grimly.

"Well, not intentionally," I demurred. "I thought—"

The boy seemed to swell dangerously. "I knew you weren't good enough for her! After all she's done for you. I ought to turn you into a salamander and hurl you into the fire!"

Unfortunately, he surely had the power to do exactly that. How could I explain?

Jewel got up and approached him. "Duban, dear, don't do anything rash. I don't think he even knew."

"Well, he *should* have known!"

She took his hand, placating him somewhat against his will. "Oh? Prince Zeyn didn't know. And did you?"

The boy looked confused. "Know what?"

"That I am Queen Nylon."

She must have changed for him, though she still looked exactly like Jewel to me. "Oh, no!" Duban blushed, then turned and hurried away. She had truly stifled his righteous rage.

And there back on the bed was the real Jewel, who had never left it. "She did have you going, Aladdin, didn't she?"

I had trouble finding words, knowing this was treacherous territory. So I took the safest course. I apologized abjectly. "I'm so sorry, Jewel. Can you ever forgive me?"

She frowned, considering the matter. Then she laughed, facing Nylon. "Debt paid?"

"Paid in full," Nylon said, making a little curtsy.

"So it's true, then. You appear exactly as I do?"

"To him, yes. Because of his great love for you."

That seemed to calm my wife down. At this point I could not be sure how much of her anger was an act. She said, "But to me you look nothing like me."

"It is because my magic has no power over you."

I shook my head, trying to make sense of this. Jewel had said she owed Nylon, for sparing her the brutal rape, but this—

"I would like to get to know you better," Jewel said to Nylon. "Why don't you come with us and be his leading concubine? Or is that beneath your dignity as queen?"

"Not at all," Nylon said. "He's *mortal.*"

"We can bring Sylvie Siren along too," Jewel continued. "To sing him to sleep." They both laughed.

It seemed I was being teased. But I liked it. "Yes, bring them both," I agreed. "At least while you're pregnant."

Jewel frowned, then called my bluff. "Done."

Was she serious? At this point, I hoped so. For one thing, it would make an honest man of me, because concubines were within bounds. And a concubine who looked exactly like my wife would not only solve my impotence, but was hardly a threat to Jewel.

"Now," said Lamprey, appearing before us in a puff of smoke, "we need to decide what to do with this castle."

CHAPTER THIRTY

We were in the great throne room.

Here sat a massive ivory throne on one end, now empty. The ivories were of creatures I had never seen before...and hoped I never would. Here and there were bits of ceiling, which had broken loose during the minotaurs' epic battle down below. The stone walls were still pocked with holes where Zeyn's stone army had broken away. Little dragons, no bigger than crows, flitted in the air above us. Some of them belched fire, but for the most part they were as harmless as birds in the sky.

The Thief of Baghdad had rejoined our group, looking very much like the sphinx who ate the swallow. Duban whispered in my ear that the thief had used a minimalizing spell to shrink much of the castle's treasure, which now lined his many hidden pockets. I only shook my head, bemused, unsure of what to do with the dastard. That he had helped my wife find her way to me was certainly something in his favor. But I did not take well to thieves in my kingdom. No doubt I would send him along his merry way with a warning to never return.

I thought it better that Queen Nylon return to my finger. I had already made one mistake in my wife's presence. I wasn't about to make another one. At least not here. Nymph Myrrh, with a bow and a small puff of smoke, returned to her magical refuge. Sylvie Siren returned to my finger, where she would remain an invaluable ally. For some reason Jewel had not wanted the alluring mermaid to reside on Duban's finger, and Myrrh had concurred. We would, of course, come to the Sirens' aid when requested, holding up our end of the deal with the beautiful sea nymphs. I would never forget Sylvie's haunting song, which would live in me forever.

Nymph Nydea stood by Sinbad's side, holding his hand tightly. He held hers in return and I sensed great love between the two. Whether Nydea faked her love or not wasn't a concern of mine. That Sinbad felt her love and was satisfied, was enough. Interestingly, as they held each other, the less she looked like Jewel and the more she looked like another very pretty young lady.

She's taking on Sinbad's wife's features, came Nylon's voice in my head. *Soon she will appear exactly as Sinbad's deceased wife.*

And does Sinbad know his wife is deceased? I asked, frowning.

On some level, yes. On another, he is in denial. Better denial than a world of hurt.

So say you, I thought, not convinced, but who was I to tell another man how to run his life?

Well, you are king, giggled the Nymph. *But in this case, I believe you are correct to step aside. Sinbad has his wife, and Nydea has her mortality and thus her chance to truly feel alive.*

I had just wondered where Lamprey had gone off to, when the tall ifrit appeared before me in a swirl of black smoke. He bowed deeply.

"Master," he said. "I was down below, ridding the castle of the zombies and stone demons. All have been banished from whence they had come."

"You are a powerful djinn," I said, impressed.

The tall being merely nodded.

Queen Nylon's words next appeared in my thoughts. *He is, after all, the rightful heir to the throne, my king.*

What do you mean?

Prince Zeyn, millennia ago, seized the throne and banished Ifrit Iften. He has been residing in the magical lamp ever since. He was a good and fair ruler, and much beloved. Our land prospered under his rule and never once did he take djinn slaves or kidnap mortal females.

This is true? I thought, surprised.

Oh, yes. But he's still bound to you, despite the freedom he presently enjoys here in Djinnland. The moment you return to the mortal realm, he will once again be at your service. Such is the curse of the Lamp.

How do we break the curse?

Only his present master can break the curse. All his previous masters were too greedy to do such a thing.

I thought about it. Her words were true. It was, indeed, a painful decision to release such a powerful secret weapon.

But let me remind you, King Aladdin, came Nylon's words again. *He may be a powerful weapon, but he would be an even more powerful ally.*

I saw the wisdom of her words. I could keep the djinn for myself and deprive him of his freedom and of his rightful place as ruler. Or I could do the right thing.

How do I free him? I asked.

Destroy the lamp.

I had tied the lamp securely to my sash, as was my habit. Now, I untied it and held it before me. Lamprey nodded solemnly, apparently accepting his fate, unaware of my intentions. Instead, I set the lamp on the flagstone floor before me and drew my sword. I didn't know how else to destroy a magical lamp, but I thought this was as good a way as any.

The Thief of Baghdad suddenly stepped forward. "King Aladdin, but what are you doing? You will destroy it."

"Exactly."

As Sinbad reached out and pulled the confused thief back, I swung my scimitar down as hard as I could. The blade struck the lamp and there was a great flash of light. I half expected the scimitar to shatter in my hands but it didn't. Instead, the lamp was gone and Lamprey took a great breath.

The breath of freedom, no doubt.

Next, he raised his hands toward the heavens and two dazzling lightning bolts shot forth from them. The lightning rebounded off the ceiling and zig-zagged crazily through the room, and where there had once been pocked-marked holes in the walls, where the demon statues had stood, there were now beautiful stone columns. And from the depths of the castle, there erupted a chorus of shouts. Shortly, men and women appeared in the throne room, all dressed in tattered clothing and blinking hard. They were an odd mix of djinn and mortal.

Lamprey turned to me and bowed grandly. I couldn't help but notice that he was floating several feet above the floor. "I am indebted to you, King Aladdin. But of my own free will. I will never forget this act of kindness, and you will always have a friend in Djinnland."

I felt Nylon squeeze my finger tenderly, and I felt a swell of emotions.

The little dragons buzzed playfully around the new king of Djinnland, erupting fire. Lamprey laughed heartily at his little friends, as more and more servants appeared in the throne room. Most looked worn-down and wasted, but upon seeing Ifrit Iften, their faces lifted with hope, and soon there was much dancing and celebrating in the great hall.

Amid the celebration, Jewel took my hand. "You did good, my husband."

"I did the right thing," I said.

"Not always an easy choice, but it's one of the reasons why I love you."

I squeezed her hand as a familiar face appeared in the dancing crowd. It was Faddy, my one-time personal djinn of considerably lesser power. He was magically juggling balls of fire, as the other servants and slaves and prisoners cleared a path for him. I watched in amazement as Faddy performed a merry routine as a magical horned instrument trumped loudly in the air next to him.

Faddy spied me and nodded briefly, before snatching one of his fireballs hurling it back into the air. He twirled once as Lamprey laughed heartily.

Nylon sensed my surprise. "Yes, my King. Your personal ifrit, El Fadl, was once the court jester until he was banned from the castle by Prince Zeyn."

"Banned why?"

"Well, rumor has it that he accidentally lit the Prince's toes on fire."

I laughed and shook my head. I always knew there was something peculiar about my ifrit. He continued to juggle and dance, and things went on like this for some time to come.

———

It was later when Lamprey pulled Sinbad and me aside.

We were in his private quarters, which, in a single wave of his hand, he had returned to its previous state, no doubt the state it had been millennia ago. Gone were the darker images and sculptures left behind by Prince Zeyn, to be replaced by fabulous works of art and beauty.

"There are many human captives that need to go home," said Lamprey solemnly. "Unfortunately, Prince Zeyn had a taste for human flesh, in more ways than one."

I shuddered at the thought. Surely the prince deserved the fire of Hades, where I hoped he'd stay.

Lamprey continued, "But I have a proposition for you." Now he looked at Sinbad. "I've received word that there lies a ship in one of our harbors, a ship from the mortal realm. A ship that needs a captain."

"I'm interested," said Sinbad. "But how did it end up here?"

Lamprey smiled. "It is, of course, a magical ship. A flying ship."

Sinbad gasped. "The Flying Dutchman?"

"But of course. It's crewed by ghosts, but it is in need of a captain." He studied Sinbad. "Are you interested?"

The sailor bowed deeply. "Would be my honor, my liege."

Lamprey nodded. "I have but one request: that you return the mortals to their homes. I will, of course, fill the holds with gold and jewels, with the hope that you will give a little to each of them. I just ask that you keep an eye on that scamp of a thief."

I said we would, and the next day, after a restful night's sleep in the arms of my pregnant beloved, I found myself boarding a majestic Dutch man-of-war, tethered to a dock and floating high above the calm water.

When the human captives had all boarded, aided by the ghostly crew, Lamprey advised Sinbad to fly the ship toward the sun, which was, in fact, the portal to the mortal realm. It would lead to the bridge between worlds and to home.

My silver ring warmed. Sylvie Siren had something on her mind. *What is it?* I asked silently.

You do plan to honor our alliance? To come to the Sirens' aid when we need it?

Of course. Anytime. I was paying only peripheral attention, being distracted by the marvelous ship.

That's good, because that time is now. I just received the news. The Siren stronghold is under siege by a horrible menace only you can hope to abate.

Suddenly I was paying full attention. "Now?"

"Of course not," Jewel responded gently. "Go quietly below-decks with your concubine." Because in my amazement I had spoken aloud.

"Dear, there's something you should know," I said, glancing at the silver ring.

She looked at me, catching on. "The Sirens?"

I nodded.

"Well, one destination is as good as another. Tell Sinbad where to guide the ship." That readily she accepted it. Maybe she preferred more adventure to a dull season at home.

We'll be there, I told Sylvie.

Thank you.

Once the marvelous vessel was untethered, it quickly rose up into the sky. As Sinbad turned the great wheel, frowning until he got a feel for the enchanted ship, Duban pulled out his lyre and struck up a merry tune. I gave them that carefree moment as I pondered what to say about our abrupt change in plans. They deserved at least a brief reprieve.

And so I took Jewel's hand and we joined the merriment, dancing together as the flying ship sailed off into the setting sun.

The End

Aladdin returns in:

ALADDIN AND THE FLYING DUTCHMAN

The Aladdin Trilogy #3
Kindle * Kobo * Nook
Amazon UK * Apple * Smashwords
Paperback

CHAPTER ONE

I t was another unproductive day.

I don't like unproductive days, especially as a self-employed private investigator living and working in the city of Los Angeles. Unproductive days meant I don't eat, pay my rent or pay my alimony. Hell, I hadn't had a haircut in months. I made it a new manly style, but the truth was I couldn't afford regular cuts. Unproductive days meant creditors would come knocking, and I hated when creditors came knocking.

Most important, unproductive days meant I didn't get to drink myself into oblivion, which is exactly what I'd been doing these past few months.

I was in my office, alone, my feet up on my old desk.

It wasn't much of an office—or a desk, for that matter. The office was just a small room with stained carpet, a couch on the far wall, where I had napped one too many times. The often-broken ceiling fan did little to disperse the hot air. A water cooler occasionally gurgled by a sink and faucet, where I kept my booze. An old TV sat on a bookshelf that was filled with novels I'd always meant to get to, but haven't found the time yet.

Not much of an office…and not much of a life, either. When I was working, I was usually tailing cheating wives, one or two of which I ended up cheating with myself.

Now, as the ceiling fan wobbled above, as the drone of traffic reached me from nearby Sunset Boulevard, I idly wondered how I could drum up more business. Perhaps start a Facebook account? Or even Twitter? Maybe both? Maybe now was a good time to see what, exactly, a Twitter was.

I hadn't a clue.

Truth was, I could barely use those new-fangled cell phones. You know, the ones that are practically a computer. Hell, I had a hard enough time with my laptop, let alone a computer the size of my palm.

I shook my head, and absently longed for the days when people actually used a land line. When a phone sounded like a phone, and not the latest Lady Gaga song.

I'd always suspected I was a man born out of time. As a kid, I often wore a cowboy hat and toy six-shooters to school—back when they allowed kids to bring toy guns to school. I longed to be a cowboy—hell, I still did. Now that was the life. No computers, no smart phones, no Twitter. Just me, my horse and the open range…

I awoke with a start.

How long I had been asleep, I didn't know. I'd been dreaming of the Wild West, of the Great Plains, of beautiful showgirls, and of whiskey. Mostly, I had dreamed briefly of long rides on my trusted horse, of its hooves pounding hard through the hot desert sand, kicking up dust a mile long behind me.

Oddly enough, as I sat up and rubbed my eyes, I was hearing just that: the sound of hooves.

"What the hell?" I mumbled.

I knew the sound of horse hooves well. Although I didn't have much, I always made a point of keeping a horse at a nearby stable, just outside of LA. Whenever I could, I took this horse out—and longed for simpler times.

The sound came again. Yes, hooves. In fact, many hooves.

"What the hell?" I said again, a little louder.

And just as I slid my cowboy boots off the desk and stood, I heard another strange sound: heavy boots approaching my office door. I'll admit, I briefly considered going for my gun located in the top right drawer, a gun I now kept nearby since an incident with a client's husband. Long story.

And so I stood there, undecided. I mean, was there really a horse just outside my door? Or had I imagined that? After all, wasn't I just dreaming of horses?

I nearly laughed. Of course, that was it.

I'd dreamed of the horses.

Maybe. I certainly wasn't dreaming of the approaching boots, which grew louder and louder. I considered again the gun in my drawer, and was just reaching for it when my office door opened.

All thoughts of my gun disappeared when I got a load of the man standing there in my office.

A man out of time, indeed.

———

The stranger was short, no more than an inch or two over five feet, and was wearing clothing that I was certain I'd never seen outside of the Renaissance fair. And even then, the clothes still seemed *off.* Just damn unusual. The man's shirt had a ruffled collar and wide stitching down the front. It appeared hand-stitched, and of a rough material that I was certain I'd never seen before.

Oh, and he wore a cape. Yes, a cape. As in Superman, minus the giant "S". It hung from his shoulder and nearly touched the ground and was embroidered with a material that looked, to my eye at least, like actual gold.

"What the hell?" I whispered yet again. Admittedly, my day had taken a dramatic turn to the weird.

Strangest of all, was the sword that hung from a scabbard at the man's right hip. Strange because it was an actual sword. A sword. Here in my office. And a highly unusual one at that. A bejeweled pommel poked up from the scabbard, a jewel unlike anything I'd ever seen before. Mostly because it seemed to be...

Glowing?

I shook my head. Surely, I was dreaming.

I was about to ask what the devil was going on when the stranger opened his mouth and...began to sing? And beautifully too…except he sang in a language I was certain I had never heard before.

And then it hit me—a singing telegram!

An old-fashioned special message. I nearly clapped, and was briefly relieved. After all, I'd been about to question my sanity. Yes, times have been rough of late. I was beginning to suspect too rough, that I'd finally lost it.

But, yes. A singing telegram.

And the guy sang beautifully…albeit in another language. Hungarian maybe?

I laughed and clapped and sat on the corner of my desk and enjoyed the show. One of my buddies had obviously set me up. Granted, I didn't have many buddies these days—and most were fellow private investigators. And, as I knew all too well, private investigators often had a *lot* of free time on their hands.

The man sang and sweated, and when he was done, I clapped again and offered him some water.

The little man frowned, scratched his head, then finally nodded. He next removed something from his pants pocket. It was a small pouch, held together with strips of colorful leather. The little man pulled open the pouch and proceeded to tap out something onto his open palm.

A white powder. Cocaine?

Next, the man did something highly unexpected. He raised his open palm to his face—and blew hard. The dust exploded out and quickly filled my small office.

"Hey," I said. "Why the hell did you do that?"

"I did it," said the man after a moment, "so that we might communicate. Can you understand me now?"

"Of course I can understand you," I muttered, coughing.

"The spell worked, I see. Very good. It's one of my own creations, in fact. The princess will be pleased."

"Spell? Princess?" I said, admittedly confused as hell. "Oh, I see, you're still in character. So, what are you, like a magician or something?"

"A wizard, in fact."

"Like Harry Potter and all that?"

"Harry Potter—" the man paused, cocked his head slightly. "Ah, you are referencing something in your popular culture. Yes, I suppose I am a little like Harry Potter and his gang of adventurers. There is, of course, one big difference."

"And what's that?"

"I'm a *real* wizard."

I grinned. "Of course you are."

"I see by your smile and easy agreement that you are using sarcasm. You are humoring me. You don't really believe me."

"I believe that you're quite a showman."

"In more ways than one, my good man."

"Now *that* I believe."

The man frowned slightly. It was almost as if he was, in fact, trying to understand me, or the intentions of my words. This day, certainly, could not have gotten any weirder.

He said, "Well, kind sir. My name is DubiGadlumthakathi—but you may call me Dubi—and I have no doubt that you will believe soon enough. You are Roan Quigley?"

I nodded, still grinning through all this madness.

He continued. "You are something called a private investigator?"

"Yes."

"And we are presently in the city of Los Angeles in the third dimensional physical realm of the planet Earth?"

I was about to grin again, but something suddenly stood out: the man sounded so...sincere. And so odd. I still could not place his accent. And had he really ridden up on an actual horse?

"Very good, then," said the man and reached inside another pocket. He extracted another pouch, this one clearly heavier than the first. I was certain I'd heard the clink of metal. And not just any metal. Gold? "We are here to hire you, Mr. Quigley."

I was momentarily caught off guard. "Hire me?"

"Of course. You do assist those in need, correct?"

"Yes, of course," I said, knowing that my grin was faltering a little.

"Well, Mr. Quigley, the Realm is very much in need of your expert services."

"The Realm?"

"Yes, Mr. Quigley. The Realm, from which we hail."

"Of course, right. And who's we?"

"Myself and the princess."

"Princess?"

"Yes, she's right outside your door. Would you care to meet her?"

"Er, I'm really quite busy—"

"I understand, which is why I've brought this."

And with that, the little man emptied onto his palm a dozen or so golden nuggets that looked, at least to my untrained eye, very real. Dubi said, "I trust this will be enough to retain your expert services?"

"Is that...?"

"Gold? Yes, Mr. Quigley, and there's more where that came from."

My mouth, inexplicably went dry, because I was certain—dead certain—that it was real gold. Real, honest-to-God gold. And tens of thousands of dollars worth of it.

"Sweet Jesus," I muttered.

"Your realm's deity, I assume?" asked Dubi.

"You assume correctly," I said, and did my best to get a handle on the situation. I sat back and crossed my arms over my chest. "So who set you up? Rick? My brother maybe?"

"Neither 'set me up,' or directed me to be here. I am here by the princess's directive only."

"Princess," I said. "Who's right outside the door?"

"Yes, with the others."

I stared at Dubi. He stared at me, smiling politely. I stared at the gold in his open palm. Then I pushed myself off the desk, and marched past the little man, who turned and followed me.

I stepped outside…and was not entirely prepared for what I saw…

———

The summer sun was high in the sky, baking the mostly empty parking lot. Mostly empty, since it was presently filled with six massive horses and four riders. Three men and one woman. Three heavily armed men, with broadswords that reached well below their boots. Even more weapons hung from various scabbards along the saddles.

They all regarded me curiously, especially the woman. I blinked in the bright light, trying my damnedest to comprehend what I was seeing, but I couldn't. For the life of me, I couldn't get a handle on what I was seeing: six horses, three warriors and a woman. Here in the middle of LA. On horseback.

And not just any woman, either. A stunning beauty who took my breath away—and who regarded me shyly.

I realized my mouth had dropped open, but I didn't care.

I was dreaming, of course. Or this was a seriously elaborate joke. Or I had lost my mind.

"I can see you're confused, my good man," said Dubi, coming up behind me. "I do not doubt that you are. Truth be known, this is a new experience for us all, too."

"What's going on?" I asked, still staring at the horses, at the weapons, at the stunningly beautiful woman sitting high above me.

"We're here to hire you, Mr. Quigley."

A very troubling thought suddenly occurred to me, one that made me doubt my sanity and to immediately swear off another drink: this is real.

"What, exactly, do you need me to do?" I heard myself ask.

"We need you to help us find a killer. An assassin, actually."

"An assassin?"

"Yes."

169

"And who did he assassinate?"

"The king, of course."

"Of course," I said. "The king. That makes perfect sense. And the young lady…?"

"Is his daughter."

I nodded, trying my damnedest to wrap my brain around what was happening to me…and couldn't.

"So why me?" I asked.

"We can explain that on the way," said the little man. "Really, we don't have much time to lose. The killer is getting away as we speak."

I felt dizzy. "I need to sit."

"We have provided you a horse, Mr. Quigley. We understand you are an expert rider."

"I…I feel sick."

"I am an expert at curing ailments, my good man. Please. We must hurry. We have a killer to catch. Will you help us?"

I looked at him, and looked at the horses—the beautiful horses. I longed to be astride such a beautiful creature. And then I looked at the princess. I sensed her sadness, her grief. Had her father actually been murdered? Assassinated?

And then she did something that warmed my heart and caused all doubt and confusion to melt away. She smiled at me.

"Yes," I said, barely able to believe the words that were coming from my mouth. "I will help you. I think."

"Very good!" said Dubi, clapping me on the shoulder and striding past me. "Then we must hurry. We haven't a moment to lose. Your mount awaits."

ABOUT THE AUTHORS

Piers Anthony is one of the world's most prolific and popular authors. His fantasy Xanth novels have been read and loved by millions of readers around the world, and have been on the New York Times Best Seller list twenty-one times. Although Piers is mostly known for fantasy and science fiction, he has written several novels in other genres as well, including historical fiction, martial arts, and horror. Piers lives with his wife in a secluded woods hidden deep in Central Florida.

Please visit him at www.hipiers.com for a complete list of his fiction and non-fiction and to read his monthly newsletter.

J. R. Rain is an ex-private investigator who now writes full-time. He lives in a small house on a small island with his small dog, Sadie, who has more energy than Robin Williams.

Please visit him at www.jrrain.com.

Made in the USA
Middletown, DE
18 July 2021